As I watched through the window, Daddy took the baby to the well. He held baby Beth over it by her heels. Mama was crying and screaming for him not to drop her child. He was like a wild madman, cursing at everyone and no one in particular. He held Beth with one hand and beat Mama with the other.

When I could no longer bear the pain, I got back into bed with Dora and Mattie. Dora hugged each of us as we lay there crying without making a sound, for fear of him hearing us. We were three little girls lost in a desperate battle to survive whatever punishment he saw fit for our Mama, our baby sister or us. Not long after, I slipped out of bed, ran to the closet and shut myself inside it. At last I felt safe. I fell into a weary, childish sleep with an old quilt draped over my head, held tightly against my ears to block out the horror outside. I awoke the next morning to hear baby Ruth crying and I smiled, thankful he hadn't killed her.

A CRY IN THE NIGHT

ONE WOMAN'S HELLISH BATTLE TO SAVE HERSELF

JEAN SMALL BRINSON

(published in hardcover as *Murderous Memories*)

St. Martin's Paperbacks

Published in hardcover as *Murderous Memories*

Published by arrangement with New Horizon Press

A CRY IN THE NIGHT

Library of Congress Catalog Card Number: 94-066755

ISBN: 0-312-95785-8

Printed in the United States of America

New Horizon Press hardcover edition published 1994
St. Martin's Paperbacks edition/April 1996

St. Martin's Paperbacks are published by St. Martin's Press, 175 Fifth Avenue, New York, NY 10010.

10 9 8 7 6 5 4 3 2 1

For my husband, Gary, and sons, Monty and Shane:
for loving me when there was nothing to love;
for seeing good in me, even when there was nothing good;
for willing me to live in spite of myself;
for all that I am or ever will be.
They are my life,
my love,
my inspiration,
my heroes
and the reason I wake up each day.

J.S.B.,

Wife and Mother

TABLE OF CONTENTS

ACKNOWLEDGMENTS

My thanks to my lovely daughter-in-law, Dana; my precious grandchild, Halee Ann; my three wonderful sisters-in-law Linda, Donna and Sherry for their love and support. And to my sister Mickie for all the laughter we've shared.

My humble thanks to my agent, Sally McMillan, for believing in me and my writing.

AUTHOR'S NOTE

This book is based on the experiences of Jean Small Brinson, and reflects her perceptions of the past, present and future. The personalities, events, actions and conversations portrayed within the story have been reconstructed from her memory. Some names and events have been altered to protect the privacy of individuals.

FOREWORD

For over two years, it was my privilege and challenge to provide therapy for the author of this splendid documentary-autobiography. I hurt with her as she made her laborious journey back to sanity and happiness.

I never treated anyone suffering from as many personality disorders as Jean Small Brinson: ambivalent emotions toward her father, symbiotic relationship with her mother, multiple personality disorder (three distinct "selves"), homicidal-suicidal tendencies, obsessive-compulsive disorder, neurotic tics and habits, psychopathic traits, identification with her father (becoming an abuser like him), even dividing her mother into two separate identities.

The reader will be enthralled by the story, the characters, the prison of insanity into which the author plunges and from which she finally escapes. Only one who has experienced such suffering could so succinctly describe Jean's hell of hopelessness, constant mental anguish, being lost in a world of hate, fear and bitterness—taking her situation to the "last straw" before regaining her sanity.

She develops a series of personas: little Jeanie the sad, lost child; Mrs. Brinson the angry bitch; and Jean Brinson, the loving wife and, later, devoted mother. Finally, with the help of therapy, she wills herself to adopt a self that can free her from the agonies of her neurotic personality, from the torment of the constant tensions created by a split conscience and wretched, Tourett-like physical agonies. This new self enables her to escape from her world of torment—not, this time, by splintering into another neurotic personality, but by becoming a controlled, healthy, even content person.

She gives due credit to the other hero of the book, her husband Gary, who with her two sons literally willed her to return to a sane and fulfilling life. The author has always been a creative and highly intelligent person, as evidenced by this fascinating account. *Murderous Memories* is both a contribution to contemporary literature and to the field of mental health.

Carol D. Wintermeyer, Ph.D.
Clinical Psychologist-Hypnotherapist

PROLOGUE

It was Father's Day. My father, naked except for his shorts, lay sprawled out on his bed. His face was pale and he appeared to be sleeping peacefully; his head was against the pillow without a case. The length of his body was spread out on the tattered sheets. I saw the brownish spots where Mama's babies had wet the bed through the years. Daddy's clothes were scattered on the floor where he had flung them. He looked like he was sleeping off another one of his Saturday night drunken stupors, but he wasn't. A small pool of blood was forming under his head. This time, he was dead.

At two in the morning, the county coroner came and made the official pronouncement. Long after his body had been removed, the room still reeked of whiskey; a nasty, foul odor lingered in the air. On the bed sheets, his blood had turned a purplish color and appeared to harden like a thin coat of paint. One of his many guns hung on two large nails on the wall alongside his working coat. The room had a deadly silence about it, but I could still sense his presence.

It overwhelmed me, engulfing my body and almost taking my breath away.

Then it hit me: I was free. Mama was free. He'd never hurt us again. I'd take care of my brothers and sisters just like Mama told me. I was a good girl and always did as Mama asked. All that mattered now was that we were free. For the first time in my fourteen years of life, I felt totally safe.

On Sunday morning, the yard was filled with neighbors, Daddy's people, his brothers and sisters; some of Mama's people were there, too. As I cooked breakfast for the children, everyone tried to be helpful—everyone except Daddy's folks. They paced the old shack with questioning looks in their hate-filled eyes. They seemed to walk in a trance, picking up his clothes, smelling and feeling them, as if by doing so he'd not be dead.

I was sorry for them that their brother was dead, but I wasn't sorry my daddy was dead. I still had my mama. She was my whole life, the reason I breathed and clung to this earth in spite of our hell and agony. It was going to be fine now—just Mama and me and the other children.

That Sunday morning was the calmest I'd ever seen. Dead lightbugs lay scattered across the porch where they had swarmed around the yellow light last night, banged themselves against the windows and fallen. I could still hear their humming ringing in my ears. I was acutely aware of my surroundings, yet I felt it was not me standing on the porch. Rather, it was some strange, skinny girl-child whose footprints echoed across the rotten boards. She paced back and forth in bare feet from the porch to the kitchen where the children were eating grits and biscuits.

I didn't know this girl. Suddenly, I felt faint, as if I couldn't catch my breath. I needed to be alone for a minute.

I walked outside, through the dew-laden watermelon and cucumber patch. Slowly, I made my way to the stalls where the mules were waiting to be fed. I loved the animals. I had a special attachment to them. I climbed the ladder, threw down hay and stood by them as they ate, petting and rubbing their beautiful heads.

"No more!" I announced. "Daddy can't ever hurt you again. I'll always take care of all of you. I love y'all."

I threw corn and slops to the hogs, petted some newborn pigs. I had wanted so to watch them be born, but Daddy said it was nasty and dirty and no child could watch. I didn't understand how giving birth to something, giving it life, could ever be considered dirty.

"Don't ask stupid questions, you dumb bitch!"

His words shot through me now as I stood and watched the pigs eat.

"No," I muttered. I wouldn't allow him to destroy my day. He was dead. Today was the happiest day of my life. The sun beamed against my face as I made my way up the foot-worn path from the stalls toward the shack. The soft, delicate white and pink scent of dogwoods in bloom filled the air. How sweet it is, I thought, as if discovering the scent for the first time. Cars drove slowly up and down the dirt road. They were filled with families on their way to church. Sunday morning turned into afternoon with a sigh and the gentle breeze of butterflies as they danced in the vegetable garden. I reached down, picked some cucumbers and held my old ragged dress up to my thighs to make an apron to carry them to the house.

I went through my daily chores as I always did, but

my mind was not there. I felt as if my body were elsewhere, too. I saw myself down the road, sitting on a pile of sand where we children played by the mounds of sawdust from an old mill. I was alone; my other brothers and sisters were not with me. I was laughing and happy and totally unafraid. He could never harm me again.

Oh, Lord. How naive and innocent is the mind of a child. How ignorant of the effects of the buried past on what lies ahead. In that moment, though, I truly believed I was safe for all eternity. I was oblivious to anything around me except the warm dirt cushioning my bare feet and the sweetest sense of freedom I'd ever known.

A
Cry In
The Night

CHAPTER
1

IN THE BEGINNING

We lived on a tobacco farm in Horry County, South Carolina. That's where it all began. I was the second of seven children for my parents, R.J. and Sara Elizabeth Edwards Small. Four girls came first, then three boys. There was Dora the oldest, myself, Mattie, Beth, Robert, Will and Tim. I often wondered how different Mama's and my life might have been if the boys had been born first and taken up for us.

Our shack was a log cabin at the end of a deserted road. The roof was covered with discolored greenish shingles. There were screens with holes covering the rotting windows. In the summer we burned alive and in the winter we froze with the cold. Mama took that shack and made it our home.

It had five rooms. Upon entering through the old rotted porch was the parlor, to the left of that was Mama and Daddy's room. Straight ahead on both sides were two small bedrooms for all us children, and at the back of the house was the kitchen. No room was separated by anything except a thin wall of boards that had spaces in them and we could see into any given room. There were no halls, just five small rooms with sparse furnishings. Clothes were stacked on boards nailed against the walls or on old trunks in Mama's room. From the outside it appeared to be an abandoned old farm structure and except for the children playing in the yards year-round—it did not have the look of habitation.

My earliest memory starts at about age three or so. I remember every detail so clearly, though I'd rather forget. I was standing at the old rusty pump near the edge of the yard. I heard voices inside the cabin. Mama was screaming—Daddy's beating her! The sound of his fists rang in my ears as he landed blow after blow. I was terrified. My hands were trembling, and the harder he beat her, the more I trembled. I wrung my hands until they were beet red, then I began to pump water furiously. I watched the water flow slowly from the yard into the muddy dirt road. I was acutely aware of the sweet scent of honeysuckles mixing with the burning heat of that hot, late August day.

Mama's screams grew louder. I saw our mangy old dog sleeping on the porch, oblivious to the torture of the woman inside. Mama's wails echoed in my ears. Quickly, I crammed my fingers into them to drown out the terror. My blue-gray eyes squinted from the sun; I was repeating the "habit" daddy had beaten me for many times. I seemed to be far older than my three years, old and weary. My tiny oval face frowned and I tried to hold back the tears, but I felt them come tumbling down as my dirty hands attempted to wipe them away. My long, blond hair was stuck to my face and neck with prickly sweat. Again I wiped and traced my fingers under my neck to rid myself of the row of dirt. Mama called it "the collard row."

"Jeanie!" she'd often call out from the cabin. "Wipe that collard row from under your neck, girl. An' put on your straw hat if you're gonna play in the sun."

Now, there were no playful orders from Mama, only screams. I saw the rickrack on the hem of my pinafore. I couldn't stop picking at it, winding it around my fingers till it was matted with knots and bound tightly. The screams settled within me, the belt zooming in the air and coming down hard against Mama. Baby Mattie was crying in her crib. The dogs were moaning and moving about restlessly as the wails penetrated their sleep. The pain was unbearable. Then, I was no longer there. I left. I went to another place. I don't know where. My sense of reality had abandoned me, except for my fascination with the rickrack on my sundress. I continued to pull and tug at it till it was torn off. The only sounds I heard were those in my mind.

"Now see what you've done, girl?" my Mama said. "My Lord. You tear off every dress I put on you. You got to stop it. Your daddy will *kill* us! You hear me?"

"Yes, Mama." I heard myself beginning to cry and tell the Mama inside my head that I will be good. But I was only a little child. Not yet three, and I didn't know what I was supposed to do.

Sometime later, I was sprung back to reality when I saw my older sister Dora coming from the barn where she had been playing with another farm child. Dora approached me laughing. She seemed to be laughing at me. Then her eyes slowly moved toward the porch where Daddy was now sitting on the steps, gripping Mama to him. Dora was five and far more brave than I. She ran to our parents and began hugging Mama, screaming at Daddy.

"Don't you hit my mama! I hate you! Don't cry, Mama!"

He let out a brutal laugh. "Aw go on, you mean little bitch! I was just playin' with your mama. Ain't that right, Sara?" He gripped her more tightly. "Speak up, woman."

Mama nodded her head. "Yeah, Daddy's right, Dora. We were just playin'. Go git your sister from the pump now and y'all git washed up for supper, girls."

That year, I started school. I dreaded leaving Mama with him and was very lonely without her all day. When I came home with Dora one afternoon in late November, I began playing on a freshly tilled piece of land behind the house, having forgotten to take off my good shoes and put on my play ones. It was a warm day for late autumn, and when I realized my mistake, I removed the good shoes and laid them at the edge of the field. Daddy was using the plow. As it grew dark, I remembered my shoes and went to get them, only to see they had been cut to pieces by the plow. Unfortunately, Daddy saw them at the same time I did. He cursed me and grabbed me by the arm. The belt zoomed from his khakis and came crashing against my backside. I saw that I was covered with red and purple welts when Mama helped wash me for bed.

She held me gently, crying without making a sound, speaking of her great love for me and my sisters. By then, little Beth had been born and Mama was raising four daughters. She couldn't stop Daddy, however, from sending me to bed with nothing to eat but a hunk of cold corn bread and water. I woke late that night and saw Mama sitting by the oil lamp at the kitchen table, sewing my tattered everyday shoes for me to wear to school. They were not made of cotton or canvas like shoes are today, but some crude form of plastic; the needle she used was huge and had tobacco twine threaded in it. All my school friends were poor, but not as bad off as we were. At least the next day all they did was laugh at me and my shoes and didn't try to pick fights with me.

I was never really sure when Daddy began his next brutal, lifelong practice of knife pitching, an "art" he dearly loved and strove to perfect. I suppose the sport of it would have been fine were it not for the fact that *we* were his targets. It started shortly after the shoe incident. Daddy lined Mama, Dora, Mattie and me against the splintered kitchen wall. It seemed like most of Daddy's cruelty centered around the kitchen, as that was where we were always summoned when he needed to further satisfy his sadistic ways. With him sitting at the table, whiskey bottle in hand and grinning cruelly, the sport began.

The first several knife pitches would be aimed several feet above our heads, in order to instill a horrifying fear within us before he really started having fun. The next pitches were inches over our heads while Mama watched and pleaded with him not to hurt her children. The more she cried and begged, the more angry he became. Then she was his target. He'd pitch the knife in such a fashion as to outline her small, delicate frame. He forbade us to close our eyes, but in the dimly lit kitchen we would squint and blink and shut them tight, praying he hadn't seen us. When the whiskey bottle was empty, he'd throw it up in the air and try to break it with the knife before it landed. His aim with the bottle was perfect more than 90 percent of the time. It was 100 percent perfect with us, his family.

Years later, but before he died, I learned that Daddy had once been the child against the wall while his father pitched knives at him, his brothers, sisters and mama. Granddaddy Julius even continued the practice on his older sons' wives after they married. Like father, like son. The knife throwing at human targets seemed to be perfected over the years, like a family heirloom passed down from father to son. When Daddy tired of pitching above our heads and outlining Mama's body with holes, he would then be ready for his climactic finish.

He'd thrust himself backward in the wooden chair, propped on its back legs, and roar with laughter. The art of the final pitches was to place the knife between his big toe and the one next to it. He'd aim, one eye closed, and pitch. He never drew blood.

Though he was usually still in a drunken stupor when this ritual was over, his appetite for violence would be appeased. If not, he'd march us girls off to bed and go back to the kitchen. I'd hear Mama screaming as he beat her with the belt. Baby Beth would be crying in the bedroom, too, and these awful sounds were more than my young mind could tolerate. It was then I began to take refuge in a closet with a quilt or old blanket pulled over my head. It became my hiding place, a secret place where I felt no one could harm me or penetrate the walls of my mind unless I allowed them. It was dark, peaceful and I could drown out the horrors of that house.

The most painful mentally, if not physically, cruel act Daddy committed that year, however, was with two-month-old baby Beth. It happened after one of his usual Saturday night brutal rituals. This time, he wanted more. He lifted the crying baby from the bed she shared with him and Mama and carried her outside into the freezing black night. Mama ran out behind him. A dim yellow light from the porch cast a shadow on him, Mama and the baby.

As I watched through the window, Daddy took the baby to the well. He held baby Beth over it by her heels. Mama was crying and screaming for him not to drop her child. He was like a wild madman, cursing at everyone and no one in particular. He held Beth with one hand and beat Mama with the other.

When I could no longer bear the pain, I got back into bed with Dora and Mattie. Dora hugged each of us as we lay there crying without making a sound, for fear of him hearing us. We were three little girls lost in a desperate battle to survive whatever punishment he saw fit for our Mama, our baby sister or us. Not long after Dora and Mattie fell asleep, I slipped out of bed, ran to the closet and shut myself inside it. At last I felt safe. I fell into a weary, childish sleep with an old quilt draped over my head, held tightly against my ears to block out the horror outside. I awoke the next morning to hear baby Beth crying and I smiled, thankful he hadn't killed her.

That old, drafty cabin burned down that same year. On a bitterly cold morning, as Mama was cooking breakfast, the kerosene stove blew up and fire began spreading through the rotting place. In minutes, there were flames all around us. All we saved was ourselves, Mama's family Bible and Daddy's rifle.

CHAPTER
2

GOOD, DADDY,
BAD DADDY

One hot, sultry day in late July when I was two months shy of being eight, I was out in the yard taking care of Mattie and Beth. We were making mudpies. Dora was in the house helping Mama with the newest baby, her first son, Robert. Daddy had gone to see his brother Albert. If we listened we could hear them cursing and laughing on Uncle Albert's front porch. It was Saturday. Mama had begun baking apple and peach pies and cooking for Sunday dinner. The delicious cinnamon smells from the kitchen perfumed the air.

It was getting late, but was still nowhere near sundown when Mama made us wash in a tub at the side of the house. I bathed the smaller girls and we all put on fresh clothes. Not long afterward, I heard Mama shouting and screaming. "Someone help me." Baby Robert was crying, Dora was frantic as she ran around trying to sooth him, and Mattie and Beth were also crying. I didn't know what was happening. Mama ran down the road to get a neighbor to help her. We started to run to the road and watch, but Mama said, "Stay in the yard or go in the house."

A truck came rumbling up the road. The driver and Mama got out after he parked on the side of a ditch. Daddy was lying there bleeding. I still couldn't see him but Mama's voice rose in fear, "He may be dying," she cried. That one thought is all it took.

I began praying to the good Lord, "Please let it be so—let him die." We could see them dragging Daddy to the cab of the truck and Mama hollered for us to mind the children. Daddy was bleeding badly. Blood was all over his tanned body and his face was a deadly white color. But he didn't die.

He stayed in the hospital in nearby Conway a few days because he'd lost so much blood. Every day before Mama came home from seeing him, I'd rock the baby in a rocker on the porch, lean my head back against the chair, stare into the distance and pretend he was dead. Then, I'd fall asleep rocking the baby and I'd dream he was dead.

"Is he dead? Is he dead, Mama?" I asked excitely when she came home. "Did he die from the blood coming out? Huh, Mama?"

"No, Jeanie," she scolded. "Now stop this."

"She's just mean and hateful," Dora said. "All she talks about is Daddy dying. Whip'er, Mama. She's mean!"

"I ain't mean!" I shouted. "*He's* mean. I hope he dies!"

"Not another word," Mama replied. "This family needs your daddy. He might be the meanest man on earth—but he puts food on the table for us all. Now you go pray for him." I did pray—that he'd die and never hurt us again.

My prayers went unanswered. He came home a few days later and somehow got even meaner. It was as if we were to blame for him being cut half to death. Daddy's version of what happened was that he and Uncle Albert drank a lot of moonshine at his brother's place and then started walking down the rut road to our house. Daddy asked his brother and his family to come have Sunday dinner with us. Uncle Albert took the invitation as an insult and he told Daddy he was no charity case and not on welfare. They both got so mad that they almost killed each other. Daddy said he finally decided they should quit and asked his brother to shake hands and forget the whole thing, saying, "It isn't our first fight, it won't be our last."

They agreed to call a truce, but when Daddy stuck out his hand to shake Uncle Albert's, he stuck Daddy with a switchblade. Cursing, Daddy looked down and saw he was bleeding. It took over 150 stitches to sew him up, starting at his neck and winding down his stomach. He refused to press charges against blood kin. Instead, he decided to take the law in his own hands. After that Daddy never left the house without his shotgun wrapped in a quilt of Mama's. He either lay in it the back of an old truck he had or in the wagon driven by a mule he often took to town. He often told Mama, "If I ever see my brother at one of the taverns, I'll kill hell out of him!"

Just a few months after that awful scene, one of the few good memories I have of Daddy took place. I got a horrible case of the shingles, only we didn't call them that. We called it the "mad itch" because of what the rash did to a person: it literally drove them mad until they scratched themselves to pieces.

My body was covered with bumps, welts and

streaks that looked like belt marks. Even my forehead and the edge of my hair line had welts, which was rare since the facial area was usually not involved. Standing in the parlor, I scratched the rashes till I bled. Mama tried to make me stop, but I couldn't. I ran to our bedroom and got on the bed. Nearly out of my mind with fever, I started jumping up and down on the mattress, screaming. Mama and Daddy came running to the room. Dora and the girls stood in the door staring and giggling like I'd lost my mind. I couldn't stop scratching, I couldn't stop jumping and I couldn't stop screaming.

"Make it stop itchin', Mama!" I shouted, digging my nails into my tortured flesh. "Mama! Help it quit!"

She tried to calm me down. "Honey, Mama's gonna help you. Stop jumpin' so I can rub you down with corn meal. Please, Jeanie! Let Mama help you, girl."

She reached out to touch me and at the same time Daddy put his arms out to me. I screamed even harder, my hands flinging in the air to fight him off.

"Jeanie!" He stared at me. "Let Daddy hold you."

"No! Mama! Don't let him touch me! He'll whip me! Make him go away. No! No! Mama! Mama! Help me!"

Mama was begging me to trust them, "Let me doctor you," she kept saying. But I could only feel fear at Daddy's presence. Wailing like an animal in agony, I jumped off the bed and headed for a closet where I could hide until he'd left. Once there, I tried to squat and pull my dress down over my knees to protect me but he was at my feet, reaching out for my body. Before I could move, he lifted and carried me to the bed, shouting for the girls to get back to the parlor. I kicked and screamed and did everything in my childish power to scratch him all over. Blood came from his arms and face where my nails dug into him.

"It's okay Jeanie," he said softly. "Daddy's gonna help you. Just trust me. Hold her down, Sara."

Even Mama couldn't do that, though. It's amazing the strength we can have when fighting for what we believe is our life. When I broke from Mama's hold, Daddy took her place. I scratched his face and then his chest. Through my reddened, swollen eyes, I saw all the scars on him from being cut and stitched. I started digging at them and even more blood came. Daddy was still trying to calm me down, holding me while Mama rubbed my entire naked body with coarse cornmeal, the only thing we poor farmers had to use for the shingles. She rubbed me softly. I begged, "Please do it harder."

She said, "I can't, your poor little body is so raw." I could hear Daddy's voice, not the hateful mean man I'd always known, but a soft and gentle father trying to help his child in sickness. He was holding me close to him as if to protect something he cared for.

Mama finished rubbing me down with cornmeal and then covered my body, even my hairline, in tallow. It was the worst odor of anything we ever used as home remedies. I felt sick to my stomach.

"Please stop," I begged. "I'm going to throw up." At some point I calmed down, and stopped scratching, screaming and fighting Daddy. He still held me close to his heart. I was filled with the fever and crying, but looking into his eyes I saw something I never saw before or after—tears falling gently down his handsome, strong face. Except for being in the arms of my Mama, never had I felt so safe.

"I love you, Daddy," I said so quietly but didn't know if he heard me. "Don't let me itch no more. Please, Daddy!"

"I won't, girl," he spoke softly. "As long as your Daddy's here, you ain't gonna itch no more."

"Daddy loves you," Mama said, as if saying words for him that he could not express himself.

That was the first night in my life I ever fell asleep without being afraid of someone beating me or my Mama in the night.

Later, I heard Daddy tell his friends that his little girl Jeanie fought him like a tiger, and that he pitied the man who married me one day.

Another of my rare good memories of Daddy occurred a few weeks before school was out. I got off the bus and ran to the field where Daddy was plowing and Mama was hoeing. I held tightly in my hand the school picture for which Daddy had paid one dollar. It was dangling on a cheap chain, about long enough to circle around one finger, and was in one of those plastic enclosures that you hold to one eye and look through to see the picture at the end. I thought I was very pretty in it, but I really didn't think it looked much like me. I ran and showed the picture to Mama, thankful Mattie and Beth were in the kitchen eating so I could have time alone to "show off".

Mama said it was real pretty and handed the picture to Daddy, who had stopped plowing now and was leaning against the handle drinking ice water. He looked through the slot, held it off, then looked again for a long time. I thought he was mad about something, maybe my hair wasn't combed right. But I was wrong.

"Whoopee!" He let out a laugh to be heard across the field. "Did'ya see that, Sara pet?"

Mama went on hoeing. "I did, R.J. Right pretty, ain't she?"

"Pretty, hell! Sara, this is my little Marilyn Monroe! Why look down that thing, Sara! Plum pretty, hell. Beautiful!"

"You really like it, Daddy?" I asked grinning. "Am I really pretty like that Marilyn Monroe picture you got on the calendar? Am I, Daddy?"

He winked at me. "Little girl, I got to be careful them movie folks don't come for you. That strawberry hair—just a shining. My little Marilyn Monroe! Well I'll be damned!"

I carried that thing around with me till I lost it years after he died. I cried when I couldn't find it. It was a great loss, as if the only legacy of his goodness no longer existed.

That same year, in summertime, he let us girls ride a donkey our landlord owned. The donkey had no bridle or saddle, so we rode bareback. I made a big mistake when my turn came by trying to get the animal to turn around. When he did, he ran toward his home and stalls, about two city blocks from our house. I was yelling for him to stop and calling Daddy to help me. I clung to the donkey's mane, hoping to stay on till he decided to stop. I was crying and scared to death. I could hear Daddy yelling, "Don't be afraid." I knew he was running as fast as he could to catch the donkey.

Daddy was only 5'10" tall, but he still seemed like a giant to me. That's because I will forever see my Daddy through the eyes of a child, filled not only with fear, but also with sadness. That summer day, as he chased the donkey and tried to rescue his daughter, I witnessed one of his finest moments. I will forever be able to see him with his shirt off, deeply tanned, wearing dungarees and barefoot, his black, naturally wavy hair flying in the breeze. To me, he was larger than life when the donkey finally came to a halt and he pulled me off. He carried me home piggyback, roaring with laughter, teasing me and saying how funny it was when the donkey took off with me clinging on for my life.

I treasure those few good memories I have of Daddy. I have to, because all the others are of the times he was a beast. At least in those few moments he was a person too— a father who, if only in those few brief moments, *did* care about his children and wife. As I later discovered, Daddy too was an abused child. His father mistreated him just as he mistreated us. I hurt for the man I called "Daddy" and who cared about me so briefly. For he never learned how to live in peace. He never learned to love.

Recalling another night, however, my memories turn back to the path of torment. Daddy became a monster again. He was reeling drunk that Saturday night. He had been slapping Mama and cursing at us children. He was standing at the front door, beating his fists against the splintered old wood. "Go to the kitchen," he ordered us all. Mama begged him to go to their room, "I'll take off your shoes and clothes," she said. But he just stood there as if no one had spoken, cursing and saying the names of men he served with in the Navy. For about fifteen minutes, he shouted out their names and then took several punches at the door. When he stopped and grabbed Mama's arm I saw that both fists were bleeding.

Later when I asked Mama about it she said that he thought he was still in the Navy in battle. I never understood that because Daddy never saw battle. He was in the Navy about eighteen months when Mattie was a baby, but he was given an honorable discharge to come home and take care of his wife, children and his Mama.

A few days later he was lying in his bed, dead drunk, when his cousin dropped by to visit for a spell. Cousin Tom tried to talk to Daddy about the tobacco crops, but Daddy's mind was on Mama and me. He had just beaten her badly and when she got the chance she had run for the woods. I knew she was going to. She had told me she couldn't take the beatings anymore and had to run away till he sobered up.

"Come on in here," he called out to me. His loud voice scared me. I began shaking. I was just outside his door. "Hurry up, girl. Now I *know* you know where she is. So you gonna tell Daddy."

He didn't know it since he was lying down, but I stood no more than a few feet from him. "No, Daddy," I managed to say. "I don't know. Mama just run—she's scared of you. Please, Daddy. Don't make me come to you."

He propped himself up on the pillows and smiled. "I tell you, Tom. Youngins—don't know how to mind you."

"Well, R.J., maybe that child *is* scared of you," Cousin Tom said. "I ain't a drinkin' man and I don't hold to it—"

"You oughta be 'shamed of that, Tom," Daddy said. "All the Small men drink—and you a Small cause your ma was my pa's sister."

Cousin Tom flipped his old felt hat around with his hands and turned. "I reckon I'd best get on home to the wife and youngins, R.J. Got to feed the livestock."

"Hell, Tom. That's what your wife and youngins are for."

When my second cousin said he was going, nothing on earth could keep me in that room with Daddy. I inched backward as Uncle Tom moved toward the door and called goodbye to Daddy. I stared till he was out the front door. Daddy was yelling.

"Little girl! Now you come on to Daddy. I ain't gonna hurt you."

"No, no, Daddy, I can't! I can't go near you. You scare me to death."

He lowered his voice but it became even more frightening. "Come to Daddy. If I have to get the belts, I'll plait 'em and tan your hide like I do your Mama's."

He was still screaming for me as I ran out of the room, out of the house and into the woods. Being careful not to make any noise, I climbed up a high tree. I tried to hide myself within the green branches. I kept my eyes glued to the back door of the house. I could still hear him calling for Mama and me. Then I heard a soft hissing sound, like a whisper. I looked around. There was Mama hiding in a thicket of briars and tall weeds. Making sure Daddy wasn't in the back door looking for or coming after us, I climbed down and ran to Mama. Her dress was torn in several places. Her hands and arms were covered with briar scratches. there were thin lines of blood against the whiteness of her skin. Talking softly, she took my hand. We started to run across the corn field. At least its height would give us safety till we reached the main dirt road.

I knew where we had to go—to our schoolhouse where Mama and I had been safe twice before. But those times, school was in session and some of the children saw us. I was so ashamed! I hated for them to see my dear Mama all bruised and crying. I told Mama, "I'm glad school hasn't started this time, so none of the children can make fun of us." We got to the school and hid under the large porch that stood high off the ground. I don't know how long we sat there, crying and holding one another, but sometime later we walked back to a neighbor's house and asked them to drive us to Mama's sister's place.

Daddy soon found out we were there and came after us, leaving Dora at home to care for the children. We all spent the night at Mama's sister's, but Mama told me later, "Even as I lay in a safe bed at Aunt Emma's, Daddy clutched me to him and said, 'I'll beat hell out of you when we get home.'" It forever amazed me that my precious Mama kept returning home to that cruel man, even to keep food on her children's plates and keep up appearances.

A few months later, on Christmas morning, Mama woke me up just before daylight. Sleepily, I opened my eyes.

"Has Santa come? Can I wake the others for our gifts?"

"No, dear," she whispered. "Your daddy ain't come home all night."

"Why not, Mama?" I asked.

"I don't know, honey. But you be quiet and let's go to the stalls to bring back the fruit and candy. I don't want the other children waking up and finding nothin'."

I followed her to the mules' stalls and went inside the lower portion of the barn. Hidden behind bales of hay were our Christmas goodies. We began hauling them up the path to the house.

It took us two trips, but finally we had all the candy and fruit in the sitting room. Daddy had bought a new yellow and green plastic couch and a green rocker and coffee table for the times when Dora would have a boyfriend at the house, but Dora had already run away in the spring of that year and we heard she was living in Florida. Mama and I took some of the fruit, nuts and rock candy and placed them in piles on the sofa. They had managed to buy cap pistols for the boys, except for two-and-a-half-year-old baby Tim. He got a red plastic hammer and a shovel, because he was always digging in the dirt. Beth, Mattie and I each got a pair of socks.

Mama hugged each of her children, saying how much she loved us and she was certain there was a good reason Daddy hadn't come home. Sprinklings of the rising sun came through the tattered curtains and lit up Mama's milky white face. She looked like the Madonna herself. She had her long black hair pulled back and tied at the nape of her neck with a red bow. She had already removed Daddy's baggy shirt, which she slept in, and put on her homespun housedress.

Later that morning, we found out that Daddy had been shot while at a tavern messing with some other man's woman. The two men had a fist fight, and Daddy walked out leaving the man on the floor. The man's brother decided to follow Daddy to his old truck. Just as Daddy put his foot on the running board to step into the cab, something hit his head and back. He spun around to see both men swinging cola crates at him. They beat him nearly to death. While trying to hold off the crates, Daddy felt a shot hit him. He passed out and fell to the ground. Although he was shot, the brothers continued to beat him with cola crates until someone called an ambulance.

He was in the hospital for exactly nine days. I can never forget that number because each time Mama had a baby, the doctor ordered her to remain in bed for nine days with her stomach wrapped tightly with bleached white flour sacks.

Again, I prayed for him to die as I rocked the baby to sleep in the sitting room and then fell asleep myself. Again he didn't die—he returned home. Again, he became far meaner than before. He had what we called the "milk leg," meaning one thigh was far larger than the other. It had something to do with him being shot in the back near certain nerves.

After that, Daddy used a cane to help him walk, since that leg was weak and he had a slight limp. That cane became his new instrument in getting our attention if we failed to come fast enough when he called. He'd reach out with the cane's crook and jerk us by the neck to his feet, causing our heads to snap back and forth. Mama, of course, was his favorite target.

In late March of the next year, while we girls were attending a Sunday night prayer meeting, I heard the frighteningly familiar sound of the cane tapping as he walked. To my horror, I looked back at the church door and there was Daddy. He was drunk and reeling down the aisle toward us. He caught my eye and with a twisted grin beckoned for us to leave church. "You go home to look after the boys," he said to me. "Daddy is taking Mama to a movie show." Later, I learned he had stopped off at some tavern, made Mama go in, then beat her all the way home because she had done it.

After that time, there were no more penny candy days, no more half-melted ice cream bars nor bubblegum, no more suggestions without saying words that meant he had some love for us. Whatever small bit of good there had been in him before he was shot was dead now. He often told Mama that he'd outlive that "sonofabitch" who shot him—and he did! That next summer, the man was shot and killed in a tavern in Conway while bragging about some "old whore" he'd slept with. He just happened to have been bragging to that whore's husband. Just for the record, the man who killed him never spent time in jail. The men of Horry County had their own rules that had nothing to do with laws or justice.

CHAPTER

3

THE NEIGHING OF THE MULES

One warm summer day we were awakened long before sunrise to work in the tobacco fields, dusting each plant with poison for bugs and worms. We rose from sleep like good little girls, Dora, Mattie and me. I was nine. We marched off in the dew-laden grass like tiny mechanical soldiers wound up by the harshness of his voice. He cursed at us as we dressed. It was "goddamn" this and "goddamn" that.

Once we'd dusted the tobacco, we marched back to the house, our bare feet covered with the wet dirt. We scrubbed and cleaned up as best we could and put on our school clothes. Then we gathered with Mama, Daddy, little Beth and baby Robert in the kitchen for breakfast. It was always the same, chocolate made into a thick paste that we poured on the plate and "slopped" with Mama's biscuits. I hated her biscuits; they always smelled like kerosene because Mama cooked on a kerosene stove. Daddy beat me many times for saying that her biscuits tasted like poison.

Often, I'd pocket mine and later give it to the old dog.

One day, Dora was extra hungry and reached for another biscuit. Cursing, Daddy slapped her small hand then he dunked the biscuit into his coffee cup and held it out to her.

"*Now* you eat the goddamn biscuit, Dora!" he shouted. "If you don't, I'm gonna ram it down your throat."

"Then you'll have to kill me first, Daddy," she said in her tiny southern accent that could become just as cold as his without warning. "I ain't eatin' that soggy thing."

Faster than lightning, he reached out, slapped her a few times and then jerked her head back by the hair. Mama begged him to stop, but Dora didn't beg. She wouldn't stoop to that; she'd rather die. She didn't cry or scream when he hit her and tried to cram the biscuit into her mouth. She clenched her teeth so tightly, he couldn't pry them open. All the while he ranted on and continued to slap her, she never even flinched. God, how I respected her for that! She wasn't weak like Mama and me. We always cried and begged like dogs.

We did not go to school that day. "Don't you *dare* allow them to leave," he said glowering at Mama. Finally, Dora wore down his anger and he decided to go on out to the fields to work. We went to work in the fields, too, in addition to brushing the yard with dried sweetgum branches till the black dirt formed patterns like ruts, helping Mama with the cooking and caring for Beth and Robert. We would have dug holes and filled them back up again if he'd said so.

His next act of inhuman indecency came around ten that morning when he returned to the house for ice water. Only the icebox was thawing and there was no cold water till the trays could freeze. He just shook his head like we were the stupidest people on earth. Then he strode out back, his dungarees rubbing hard against his legs. We ran to the door after he'd gone and edged outside to watch him. There was an electric fence in the edge of the yard surrounding the hog pen. He looked at it with a devil-like wonderment, his deep blue eyes squinting as a small grin formed on his lips. Then he yelled, "Mama" and we marched down the steps with her as she moved toward him. In an instant he grabbed her hand, then clenched the electric fence in his other fist. A cruel farmer's trick when he wanted to grab the pigs or mules to punish them. The electricity shot through the hand holding the fence and went into the person or animal being held. I never knew how it worked, but it did. Mama started screaming. The more Mama cried and begged him the more he laughed watching her and enjoyed his cruelty. I was not prepared when her delicate voice screamed out, "You mean sonofabitch, R.J.! You whorehoppin' piece of dirt! Why don't you just die?"

He stared at her and he pushed her down grinding her body in the dirt. All of us cried and begged as he beat her and broke many of her ribs. "Now will you ever curse me again?" "No, no," she shook her head. Yes, she was sorry. Yes he was her man. Yes, he was a sonofabitch.

I couldn't bear to see him hurting my Mama anymore. I ran to the outhouse and hid in the corner with my face buried in the old wood. I plugged my ears to try and drown out the sound of pain. I was too scared to move. I just lay in that old outhouse, rotten and filled with a disgusting stench that gripped at my tiny belly and made me sick. Finally I peeped through the cracks. Dora and Mattie were helping Mama to the back steps. I was almost thankful, thinking he was finished till the next time. He wasn't.

I kept my eyes glued to him as he moved swiftly to the side of the house where Dora's kitten lay. He reached down, picked it up high over his head and began swinging it around and around. There was no warning. No time for fear or pain. The kitten swung faster and faster and Daddy let go and it went sailing in the air till gravity took over and sent it plunging into the side of the house. In an instant the kitten was dead, its guts spattered on the house. I could see its small head torn half off by him. The children screamed but I lost all awareness of them. I just lay in the corner, covering my ears with my hands and burying my head in the darkness of the outhouse, so I could not feel the kitten's pain or my sister's or my own. Then it was over, as if nothing but the blissful normality of a family lived there, and I was aware of Mama taking my hand and leading me into the house for dinner.

"It's gonna be all right," she assured me as she held me close to her apron for a second. "One day he will die. The Good Lord will see to it. Then all this will be just horrible memories—memories that we'll forget in time. Time heals all wounds, honey. You remember that."

"You promise, Mama?" I wept. "All 'uv'em?"

"All," she whispered. "Now set the table."

"I love you, Mama. I'd die for you, Mama. I would."

"I know. I've always known," she said softly.

Through the years of torment no matter what alliance we had formed to combat his cruelness, we always fell short of our goals. Just when we thought we could let our guard down and relax like normal children, he'd have another game plan. We never stood a snowball's chance in hell.

We were clearing the dishes to be washed when I heard him hollering in the front yard. I started running through the parlor to look out the window. Mama called to me, "Stop lookin." But I couldn't. I knew what he was doing. I'd seen it countless times and, no matter how much pain it caused me, I couldn't stop staring in terror.

He was beating the mule mercilessly! The mule neighed in high pitched terror. The animal's head was thrust backward in a motion to get away from the real beast. Daddy, the true animal, was holding a "twitch" in the mule's mouth. A twitch is a piece of hickory wood, crammed into the hole on the mules bits. The bits are placed in the mouth and the hickory wood is twisted around several times to force the bits to cut into the skin on the lips. It caused thick foam to drool in wads on the mane.

The terror, the horror! The mule turned in circles and her neighing grew so horrible I felt the pain go through me. Now Daddy beat her with an iron crossbar used for hitching mules. It crashed against her neck and sides, drawing hunks of flesh from her body. Her blood spattered on the porch. It was almost black, and thick looking. Finally, having worn himself out, Daddy put the crossbar down, rubbed the mule's head, and petted her like a prized possession.

So long as I breathe I shall never forget his words nor the cruel smile on his ruggedly handsome face.

"Now you ready'ta go to work, girl? Then you can have water."

I knew I would always hear the horrible sound of the mule's neighing in my mind, and feel the terror of her pain in my own heart.

CHAPTER
4

HABITS

There was never a time in my life when I didn't have what we called "habits." Sucking my thumb until I was in school, blinking my eyes furiously, uncontrollable twitching of my head, rapid breathing, slinging my right hand up and down—so many habits! For every one I developed, Daddy found a new way to punish me. The more pronounced my habits became, the worse the beatings got.

The meaner Daddy grew, the more afraid I grew and the more habits I developed. My constant companion was fear—fear of my Daddy. The person I should have been allowed to trust with my life, I couldn't. I saw him beat the other children for misbehaving, but he saved his greatest abuse for me and Mama, perhaps because he saw our special bond. I was a nervous child, afraid to even breathe in the presence of the man I loved, hated and wished dead.

Early on in life, I learned the rule of our household. Speak only when spoken to unless Daddy was sober and smiling. We could not under any circumstances try to hug Daddy unless he asked for it. We were never allowed to talk at the table and always had to eat what you were given. I did not realize it then but Daddy was just carrying on the beliefs and values of the men in his family. Wives and children were regarded as possessions and a man had the right to beat them until they died, if he so chose. Whores bore the Small men's bastard children (Daddy was the father to three that we knew of) who were entitled to the same rights as children born in wedlock. Better, actually. Whores and bastards were not beaten. They were "things" which you bragged about as you sat on the barn bench drinking with your menfolk friends.

Wives were to be kept pregnant in the summer, barefoot in the winter and always bore signs of beatings. This was the ultimate glory for the men in his family and showed the others that he had "done his homework." The men in the family didn't attend church; they whorehopped and got drunk instead. They made their children go, but if Mama or another wife went to church, she was beaten upon returning home. In Daddy's or one of the other men in the family's twisted minds, going to church meant the woman had been to bed with a deacon or snuck out with the preacher. Thus the tradition of my daddy's people became the cornerstone of the hate and torment that lived and grew within me with each passing day.

At school, my teacher was always yelling at me, usually for the same offenses.

"Now Jeanie," she'd start. "How many times do I have to get on you? Why do you keep doing it?"

"I don't know, Miss Johnson," I'd mumble.

"Now Jeanie, why do you insist on putting those

dots at the end of a sentence that's a question? You can't put dots *and* a period in a question mark sentence."

"Stop blinking your eyes."

"Stop noddin' and shakin' your head."

"I'm going to march you home to your daddy if you don't quit laughin'."

"No! You don't have a cold! Those are just bad habits!"

"Those habits are ugly! You look retarded!"

"Beat me, Miss Johnson!" I cried out. "But please don't tell my daddy."

A quizzical look would appear in her eyes. "Why not? Are you scared of your daddy?"

"Oh no, ma'am!" I said quickly. "He just hates my habits. But he's a good daddy. Honest."

"Very well, Jeanie. Get me a switch; I'll punish you."

I ran to the woods behind the tiny school and fetched a switch, hurrying back to take my punishment. At my request, so my classmates wouldn't see them, Miss Johnson always put the lashes on my behind or backside. The truth was, if Daddy saw them he'd do two things— beat me again, after which he'd haul off to school and curse at my teacher. He'd done that on several occasions when Dora had been whipped. Then we were really the laughing stock. I'd rather the teacher kill me than him know I'd been punished.

One might expect I'd have learned from all the beatings, but I didn't. I couldn't stop the "habits" though, and the next day Miss Johnson would light into me again.

"Don't blink your eyes, girl!" she'd scold. "Stop makin' those stupid dots all over your paper! Where is your mind, girl? Are you really here with us? Are you stupid?

Maybe I should march you off to your daddy."

"Oh no! Please, Miss Johnson!" I'd cry out. "I'll try harder. Honest I will. I'll hold my hands behind me. I'll stop doing everything wrong." But, of course, I couldn't.

CHAPTER
5

UNSAFE AGAIN

After Daddy's death, Mama could no longer raise us children on a sharecropper's tobacco farm, so she moved us to Charleston. My sister Dora was still in Florida, where she had been living when Daddy died. We heard she had run away over a year earlier with some man. But in September, just months after Daddy died, she returned, several months pregnant. The following May she had a darling baby girl whom I loved like my own. Dora and I had never been close, but Dora did let me care for her baby while she worked. As far as I was concerned, Mia was *my* child—the first thing I could call my own.

Even though Dora worked as a bartender after the baby came, not even the pooling of all our paychecks could pay the bills and keep the children in food and clothes. Having lived on a farm all her life, Mother, which is what we called Mama after we moved to Charleston, never knew what it meant to pay rent and utilities. In our financial state, it was impossible.

Mother finally decided she had to make an awful decision. If all the children were to eat and the rest of us still survive, she had to put my three brothers and two younger sisters into a children's home. Though it almost killed her to do it, she put them in a home in Greenwood, South Carolina. We got an old car, took them there and visited them twice a month.

Meanwhile, I was growing up. I began dating and drinking a few beers to enhance my usually somber moods. I would dance all night, go home and sleep a few hours and still work at the dime store early the next day. Young men flocked to me, telling me how beautiful I was. I learned quickly to be a good dancer, but I didn't want to be just *good*. No, I had to be different. Where all the couples were doing the shag, I took that move and incorporated it into my version of the jitterbug. Other couples would leave the floor to watch me and my partner, forming a circle and clapping while I danced with whoever happened to be the best male dancer in the place.

I thought my demons, like Daddy, were dead. At last, Little Jeanie was on her own. People complimented me. They stopped me on the street to say how beautiful I was. I couldn't believe it. My feet still had tobacco stains on them, and people were telling Mother I should enter beauty contests!

For a while, I was almost happy. I lived for the nights at the beach or some other "joint," dancing and being with whoever was my current beau. Of course, I felt the need to be accepted; I felt it very strongly—perhaps even obsessively.

Then, when I was twenty-one, something unexpected happened: I met Gary Brinson. Mother was working as a cocktail waitress in a club downtown. I went to see her one night and was sitting there on a bar stool talking to her when she introduced me to him. I took a long look at him. His thick blond hair kind of fell over his brow; his skin was like dark honey from being tan. Just looking into his huge brown eyes, ringed with the thickest and longest eyelashes, made my heart pound. The intensity of my desire scared me. Even though the fear of the unknown was there, I felt compelled to get to know him. Without thinking of reasons or consequences, I felt I *had* to be with this person. We soon began dating, and my feelings for him grew even deeper.

When he made love to me, I returned that love with every fiber inside my young body. It was heaven. Now the shame of sex was gone and in its place was the wondrous feeling of knowing we were like two souls united. Nothing could ever separate us. He seemed to feel the same way, and we became inseparable.

It was almost inevitable that I eventually became pregnant. At first, though he gave me a diamond ring and I wore it proudly, I refused to marry him. I was afraid he was being kind for the unborn baby's sake. Only when I was almost five months pregnant, and he still seemed to love me, did I finally say yes. By then the feeling of that tiny thing growing inside me, a part of Gary and myself, was wondrous. I wanted to make our love last forever.

We were married that September and our love, like the baby, continued to grow. This was the happiest time of my life. To me, there was no greater pleasure on earth than to have Gary come home from work, take a shower with me and to have us both feel my bulging abdomen. It was still wondrous making love, even when the baby felt "knotted up." Gary would rub me gently, then, till the baby settled down. By this time, I worked at another dime store, where I stayed until two weeks before my due date. I was still so tiny, it amazed people when I said my baby was due at any time. I had a glorious pregnancy, spending my spare time planning all the wonderful things I would do as a mother.

Monty came into the world on February 15, after only five hours of labor. I wish I could say I was brave during labor, but I was not. The pains were terrible. I told Mother if she loved me to please kill me. I did not want to suffer through that hell! Even though I was in a Catholic hospital and surrounded by nuns, I cursed and ranted until I was taken to the delivery room.

When little five-pound, three-ounce Monty arrived and they laid him on my stomach, I immediately became afraid, despite my joy at becoming a mother. A fear began to gnaw at my guts—not the old fear, but a brand new, greater one. This new fear tore at my very soul. During my three-day stay in the hospital, I had to have a nurse with me every time they brought me the baby. I was not able to breast feed or hold my baby alone. A horrible thing was happening. An old fear. A new fear. Both had ruined what should have been one of the happiest times of my life.

I had always felt that I wasn't "normal," not like my sisters and Mother or any of my friends. A constant feeling of fear dwelled in me, a feeling that something bad was always about to happen. I didn't realize what caused it, but it was there and I sensed it would destroy me in the end. This fear served to remind me that at any given moment fate had the power to destroy my mind.

The only thing I could compare to this awful feeling was how I felt when riding in a wagon pulled by mules, with Daddy, when I was a little child. He'd beat the mules to make them go faster, and the wagon would hurtle down the dirt roads at a speed that scared me to death. I'd plug my ears to drown out the sound of the mules neighing from pain or the rusty wagon wheels grinding against the spokes. I was petrified that the wagon would overturn, especially when he rounded a bend or turned quickly onto another road. Not having a closet to hide in, I'd lie down, bury my head in my ragged dress and start tearing at it. By the time we returned to the house the dress would be torn to pieces and have to be thrown away. Then I'd get a whipping from Daddy, unless he made Mama do it.

When Monty was less than two months old, I felt that same kind of fear again, only magnified a thousand times. One day, as I sat in a rocker feeding him, I kissed his tiny fingers and pressed his delicate body against my breast. I could feel the warmth of new life breathing in him. Then, suddenly, I began to sweat. My entire body shook, and my mind whirled with the awful thought that I was going to hurt him. I could not stop thinking this way.

"Throw him against the wall and kill him!" my mind screamed. I had to get him back to the crib—but how? I was too scared to stand up and walk with him in my arms I tried to speak, but no words came. Holding Monty, I inched myself to the floor, laying him on a blanket. Slowly, I got up on my knees and pulled the blanket inch by agonizing inch until I was across the room beside his crib. The floor was like ice. It was February. Winds howled outside.

I stood gazing down at my baby, whom I dearly loved, my thoughts on fire. How could I safely get him into the crib without lifting him? If I picked him up, I felt like I would throw him against the wall. I started to shout aloud, "Oh, God! Help me, God! God, God, God! Help me! *Please* help me. Let me die. Don't let me harm my baby! If you're a good God, you'll strike me dead so I can't harm my baby!"

I paced the room, then the whole apartment. Frantic, frenzied, my mind was burning. I was losing my mind; I was going insane!

Fear had a stranglehold on me. I took small, mincing steps toward the spot where my precious baby lay. "Just let me make it to him," I prayed. "Just let me keep my sanity until I reach him and lay him in the crib."

Then I was there, staring down at his helpless form, the baby who needed me desperately. I leaned over, bending my knees, and lifted each corner of the blanket. Slowly I brought the corners together, tying opposite ends to form a knot. The baby never made a sound.

I wrapped him gently in the blanket and began to lift him into the air like a fragile package—slowly, carefully. I lifted faster, higher and saw the package swinging over the crib. But I couldn't trust myself. I lowered it and loosened my grip. Jumping back quickly, I was startled to hear the doorbell ring. I leaned back over the crib, untied the knots and laid the blanket on each side of Monty. Only then did I see his eyes. They were slightly open and he was smiling and making coo-like sounds.

I fell to the floor, suddenly limp. I heard Mother calling to me, heard her key open the door and her footsteps as she came up the stairs.

"Oh, God! Are you all right, honey?" she asked, helping me to my feet. "What happened? Did you fall?"

"Help me, Mother!" I sobbed. "Please hold me. Tell me I'm not crazy."

She knelt by me as I huddled against the crib. "Oh, my beautiful girl. No, my darling. You're not crazy. Why on earth would you think that? Come, let me help you to the bed. You need lots of rest. Hold onto me; I'm here."

I lay on the bed, holding her hand. I told her what had happened, about my horrible feelings. I thought maybe, being the mother of seven children, she'd know what I was going through. Instead, she stared at me in the strangest fashion I'd ever seen. Her beautiful Cherokee and Irish face was solemn. With her high cheekbones, she normally had the face of a piece of sculptured art. Now her face was taut and drawn.

"Mother!" I cried. "Please don't look at me like that. What's wrong with me? I need you, Mother. Please."

"I'll always be here for you." Her tone had changed. It was now firm and authoritative. "But as long as I'm living, don't you ever tell me again you want to hurt my grandson. I don't know what's wrong with your mind as far as the baby—but whatever it is, get help! Get help right away. And till you do, I'm going to stay here with you and Gary to watch the baby." I thanked her as if she were my savior. Together, we talked to Gary that night and he agreed I needed help.

Later, I called Dora. "We're all crazy," she said. "If you go to a psychiatrist and tell him how you're afraid you'll hurt your baby, he'll have you shipped to goddamned Egypt, locked up and I'll throw away the key." Dora didn't understand that I couldn't help my feelings, couldn't control them. Even with Mother staying in our apartment, the hellish fear that I could hurt Monty consumed my every waking moment. It was hardest when everyone else was sleeping. Then, my baby had no one to protect him from my warped mind and I had no one to keep me from self-destruction.

I should have been the happiest woman alive. I loved my husband and he loved me. I was the mother of his child, a son he so wanted. Telling my husband of my sickening fears of wanting to harm our son was one of the most horrible things I had ever done. I saw such hurt in his eyes.

From then on, I couldn't allow myself to pick up Monty. I had to care for all his needs while he lay in the crib. The fear torturing my brain, I'd stand as far off as I could and reach for the bottle to feed him, or bath him with small amounts of water. As my hands moved toward his tiny throat, though, I would became so afraid I'd jump back and begin hyperventilating. Then I'd regain some courage from somewhere and quickly I'd reach in the crib, kissing him, telling him of my deep love for him. The next second I was crying, out of control, begging God to let me stop living in fear or allow me the peace of death.

Once again, my life became a long, tormented road, just as when I'd been a small child. I talked it over with Gary and Mother and decided to see a therapist. Two months later, though, I stopped. It just wasn't helping me. Gary and I insisted that Mother return to her apartment. I knew I had to learn to control the fear myself, or die trying.

My existence became a living hell, swinging from its formerly fragile hold on sanity toward total insanity. Monty was my sole connection with reality; yet I had somehow linked him with Daddy and he was at the core of the fear and rage that was dragging me down into the netherworld. Mother would visit, hold me and tell me, "Now, forget him. Your daddy's dead. Bury him and let yourself live."

And like the good daughter, I'd press my face to her chest and say, "Yes, Mother. Don't worry. I'm much better."

Lies! How could I lie to Mother? I felt so ashamed. How could I tell her that my days were spent standing over my baby's crib, that when he cried I'd run outside? How could I tell her I'd written a letter, hidden in my purse, to be opened in case I died, in case I killed myself?

I was doing the only thing I could to keep from hurting my son—I didn't hold him unless others were present. Most days, I huddled in the closet with a blanket over my head. The darkness allowed me to escape once again, as it had so long ago, but still it wasn't enough. I was sinking.

Through all this, Gary was the object of both my violent outbursts and my desperate cries for love. Gary came from a family as large as mine. There were six girls and two boys, and Gary had a twin sister. Though I adored his whole family, I became very close to his oldest sister, Libby. She was nearly five years older than me, but we had so many things in common. By the time Monty was born, Libby already had two children. Gary and I lived in the city and Libby would come on Thursdays to pick Monty and me up and take us to her home in the suburbs where she'd try to teach me how to bake marvelous cakes and cookies. Libby, like all the Brinson children, was olive complected and beautiful. Their father had the same coloring; not one of the eight children was fair-skinned like their mother.

We played cards at each other's houses, all his sisters, their husbands, Gary and I. It seemed the girls were always having some sort of get-together. I lived both in fear and awe of those times. I longed to become a part of my husband's family, but I feared that the other "parts" of me would appear and they would think I was crazy. When none of the other then-emerging parts of my splintered psyche surfaced at our gatherings, however, I became more confident in seeing Gary's family. So for the first three years, before our second son was born, we had many good times.

But something was happening to Mrs. Gary Brinson, wife and mother. Gary enjoyed his beer after a hard day's work in the sun as a carpenter. The day came, however, when I couldn't stand the sight of the can in his hand. It became a battle between us. I remember one typical scene when I lashed out at Gary.

"I hate it when you drink, Gary. You remind me of Daddy," I said accusingly.

"I'm not your Daddy, Jean," he said. "I would *never* harm you. I couldn't. I'm not that bastard."

"But you drink too much, and so did he," I said.

"Jean, you have to begin to separate the past from the present." He got another can of beer and sipped it.

"Oh, go on and drink the world dry, you stupid sonofabitch." I called him every curse word I knew, vulgar, degrading things that I thought women never said. I spit in his face. "Leave me alone!"

During times like this, I hated the sight of him. I'd become so angry fighting with him, my body would grow weak. Sometimes, I couldn't even walk straight. Then, it would suddenly be over. I'd run to my room and bury my face in the pillow to hide my shame, crying, "I hate myself. I want to die." I often wanted to take a knife and cut my body to pieces. Was I possessed by some evil spirit? Was I Daddy reincarnated, a devil with invisible horns?

After the feelings of intense shame had subsided, this particular time, I went to Gary in the kitchen and tried to talk to him. He walked away when I tried to touch him. "I don't know what happens to me, Gary," I said.

"Me either, Jean," he'd answer. "You're so many different people—all kinds of personalities in one. Monty and I never know what to expect."

I hugged him tightly, but felt his body reject me again. My voice became childlike. "Love me, Gary. Help me. Please, Gary," I pleaded.

"It would be a sin to make love to you now, Jean. I can't explain it, but you're a little girl right now. It would be like raping you. Like raping a child of nine or ten. An hour ago, you were a woman, but now you're this little kid. Sometimes, I don't know *who* the hell you are. Make up your damn mind! Are you my wife? Monty's mother? Or are you ten different people we don't know?"

I shook my head furiously. "I don't know, Gary. I don't know. I have these uncontrollable fears. I hate myself, but I'd die for you and Monty."

After a while, when both my body and mind had succumbed to total weariness, Gary saw me hunched over in a corner. Coming over to me, he held me like a small child and didn't say a word while I wept and wept. Later, perhaps before went to bed, Gary finally spoke.

"Where do you go, Jean?" he asked softly.

"What, Gary? What do you mean?"

"When you go into your rages and then wilt and go into our bedroom closet with a blanket over your head. You fall asleep in there. Where do you go, honey? In your mind, where are you, Jean? Tell me so I can help."

"Back there, Gary. On the farm. When I was a little girl. I go there like a child because I'm safe there. Little Jeanie is where I go."

"You *become* a child?"

"Yes, Gary, I can't help it. I know what I'm doing—I know I'm acting like a scared child—but I can't stop. I feel so safe when little Jeanie comes and rescues me."

And so the battle within me went on. There was another person that I sometimes became, however, someone totally different. At these times, I would give in to my urges to laugh and be free and do all the silly things I'd not done in years. I'd play the music I thrived on—rock and roll—loud. I'd take Monty's small hand and we'd dance all around the living room while Gary drank and laughed at us. I'd dance with Monty till he was in tears from laughing so much. Then I'd hold him in my arms, still dancing around the room, twirling him in the air, kissing my precious son and it would be a grand and joyous time for hours.

Whether I was the child, the bitch or the free spirit, the culmination of these countless days and nights was always the same. I'd get severe chills, even in August; I'd become so weak I'd have to sit in the hottest water I could in order to stop shaking. Back in bed, little Jeanie would come and take me to a safe place where no one was allowed to enter. I'd rest peacefully with her in "our little world."

Like a yo-yo, up and down, I could be the good mother, the faithful wife or the merry dancer filled with love and laughter. Then the bitch would come and try to destroy me, destroy my marriage, destroy Monty. She'd come like a hurricane, with a force no one could tame. I'd grow meaner and meaner and even more ashamed of being alive. My greatest fear had become reality. I was becoming what I hated and feared most: Daddy.

6

A Place of Screams

Finally, my problems became too much. On a chilly day in late October, since Gary and I couldn't afford prolonged treatment, I signed myself into the state asylum. I sat on a rotten chair in the corner of an office and listened while the doctor who was admitting me fired questions.

"Name? Age? Married? Children? Husband's name? Children's names and ages? Date of birth? Religious preference? Mother's maiden name? Father's name? Living or dead? Make up your mind—Mrs. Brinson—is he living or dead? Why are you here? What's the matter? So you're sick. I see."

Degrading, I thought. Inhuman. The State Asylum! How low had I sunk?

The doctor was in her late fifties, ratty gray hair in a nappy bun. She had huge colorless eyes that looked right through me as if I were naked. Her white uniform was filthy with food and coffee spots, and I noticed the dirt under her unkempt nails. Her teeth were yellowish with spots of lipstick smeared on them. I quickly noticed they were dentures with phony pink plastic gums. As she talked they made annoying clicking sounds against the gums. She adjusted her black horn-rimmed glasses, peering at me over them.

"What did you say, Mrs. Brinson?" she asked.

"Can I call my husband?" I replied sleepily and tired. "May I call Gary and my sons? Please?"

"Do you realize where you are? It's the State Asylum, Mrs. Brinson. You've never been here before, have you? You're in for a great experience, dear. This is the last stop on your road to hell."

"But I have rights!" I pleaded. "I am not committed. I signed myself in. I'm free to leave. Right? I've changed my mind. I want to go home. I'm going home. Open that big door, I have to go home."

I heard what she was saying but it didn't make sense to me.

"Rights? You have no rights here, dear. You are committed—all patients are. You and your husband and your doctor signed the papers. We have rules here. Not even the governor himself can get you out of here for thirty days."

"Thirty days? Oh, God! Help me! I've made a big mistake! Are you listening, God? Help me! Please! I'm not crazy!" I told her. "I'm just sick."

She roared. "They all say that. The bitches swear over their dead mother's grave that they are sane, and we are the ones who are insane, but *they're* insane. Take it from me, dear."

"No—I'm not insane—I'm not like them!"

"The sooner you admit it, the sooner we'll get along.

If we get along you'll find that it works much better for both of us." She leaned over the desk closer to me. Her foul breath nauseated me. "I hate weak people. The weaker they are the more disgust and contempt I have for them."

I began rattling my head off about how strong I was, telling the doctor how I would move the furniture around the house when my husband wasn't home.

"I'm not weak. Really, I'm very strong. I want to go home now."

She snapped, "Not that kind of weak, Mrs. Brinson! So just shut—shut the hell up!"

I lost all control then. I heard screams that seemed to echo down the cold gray corridors. I felt myself moving about the small room, hands clinging to the coldness of the gray painted concrete walls. I wished the screaming would stop! Why couldn't I drown it out?

However, the screams were mine. The burning and the fear in my guts were mine. I couldn't stop screaming! Oh dear God, what if I never stopped? Would I live here forever?

Two orderlies entered the room and grabbed me. They were talking to the doctor, but all their words became muffled, as if they were in a drum. I felt a gag being put on my mouth and tied behind my head. My eyes were shut tight. Then I was dragged down the hall to the nurses' station. Immediately I heard shuffling of feet and non-coherent sounds coming from patients. I opened my eyes and saw the blur and horror on their faces. They were twisted in a raging kind of laughter, laughing and pointing at me.

"Thorazine. Two hundred milligrams," I heard the doctor tell the nurses who had gathered around me. "And a shot of Valium. If that doesn't work we can always shut her up with the Phenobarbital. It would work wonders on this one."

I had never taken a tranquilizer. I didn't even know what the medications the doctor ordered were. Someone removed the gag while they shoved pills down my throat and soaked me with a glass of water. Immediately I felt drowsy. I had this urge to lie down and sleep forever, but even with the pills the fear I felt would not allow me to find peace.

They grabbed my arms and shoved me face down against the counter and put a straight jacket on me. I was bound so tight I could feel my heart throbbing. They dragged me down the hall to a ward where at least twenty other women slept. I was aware of being slammed into a cot and someone putting a blanket over me. Then I drifted into an oblivion where I had nightmares about my grandma. My mother's mama had spent the last thirteen years of her life in this hellhole. On a visit home she suffered several strokes and died. I wondered if she'd ever slept in the cot I was using. I thought perhaps she had, and I gained a certain sense of calm from that.

Later that night, I opened my eyes and saw a woman with stringy white hair and glassy blue eyes trying to get into bed with me. The gag had been removed from my mouth, but I didn't scream. I just stared at her until she left, mumbling words known only to her demented mind.

Morning came with horrifying reality when several huge women orderlies who paced the halls ordered everyone to strip and head for the showers. "Move in a single file from each direction." We entered the shower room, two at a time. In pairs, we occupied one stall with a shower nozzle on opposite sides of it. We paraded naked with a dingy white, thin towel draped over one arm and underpanties held tightly in the other hand. I was freezing and began to have chills. I prayed I would make it to a hot shower before the trembling came full force.

Like Mother, I suffered horrible chills. Mine had begun in childhood. No doctor could explain them. They came without warning. Mostly they came when I was depressed or nervous. Suddenly I would begin to shake uncontrollably. The only thing I ever found that stopped them was plunging into a tub filled with hot, skin blistering water. At home I slept with two heating pads, one braced between my knees, the other pressed against my stomach. Even the electric blanket wasn't enough. I would pile quilts on top of it. I'd wake in the night, washed down with sweat.

Now I got into the shower expecting relief. Instead I was shocked. The water was like ice. I started screaming and begging, "Please turn it off."

"A hot bath!" I begged. "Please. A hot bath. I'll die!"

"Where the hell do you think you're at? The god-damned Hilton?" a frizzy red-haired orderly shouted at me.

"I'm freezing! Please, lady! Help me! For God's sake!"

She held me under the water as I tried with all my strength to avoid the cold spray.

"Freeze, bitch! Die for all we care. You crazy bitch!"

Then I thought of something. If I said I was crazy she would stop; so I told her I was insane like all the women. I promised to do anything—crawl if I had to, wipe her filthy behind if need be—anything to get away from the shower. Nothing helped. My pleading fell on deaf ears. My teeth chattered, my skin turned blue and my face became rigid and solemn. Then I began to hyperventilate. My body shook out of control. Through it all I could see the naked old women gathered around my stall with their old wrinkled breasts hanging against their chests. I became frightened at the sound of their hideous giggling.

Suddenly, a dark haired woman came in. Everything was blurry, I couldn't see who she was. "Please help me," I mouthed, but no sound came to my lips. I heard her voice shout at them.

"Outa my way, you old naked bitches! Turn off the water, Martha! Now, you damn bitch!"

"Want to make me, Annie?" the orderly said.

"Don't have to, Martha. You love candy and smokes too much to disobey me. Now move, bitch! And get me a paper bag. She's hyperventilating, and she's turning blue. She'll die! Get me the friggin' paper bag!"

Within a minute or so I was handed the paper bag, but I couldn't control my hands to use it properly. Annie wadded the end and pressed it over my mouth. Slowly I began breathing normally. She helped me from the shower and to a ward to dress. A few days later, I was shocked when Annie told me she was a regular in the state asylum.

"I come here yearly for my vacation," she laughed.

"Vacation from what, Annie? Hell?" I asked.

She said her husband was a Baptist preacher in a small southern town. He was old and believed in hellfire and brimstone. Annie shrugged, "I believe in living and having a good time." Her husband had announced at Sunday services she was in the state hospital and she cursed him with every name in the book. I never really knew what Annie's mental problem was, but I felt a kindred spirit with her and was forever thankful to God for her help. Had it not been for her, I think I would surely have succumbed to institutionalization and to insanity.

Even with her friendship, it was still difficult not to fall apart. The hospital was filled with lost souls, screaming out the terror of their twisted minds. Women lay naked on the cold floor, their excretion between their sagging legs. They moaned in agony and cried out names incoherently. They slept in their own stench. One woman who had vaginal cancer bled as she walked and fell on the concrete floor. No one helped her.

Susan, a young woman in her late twenties, was paralyzed and confined to a wheelchair. Annie and I took turns feeding her when her plate was sent up. Sometimes it wasn't. Then Annie would raise hell and make them get Susan food. When she needed to urinate, we lifted her frail body from the wheelchair onto the toilet and wiped her. Every night we bathed her, and put her in the cot to sleep. The nurses seemed to loathe us for that. Annie said, "They love to see patients helpless and in torment." I prayed they'd all burn in hell.

People didn't act the hysterical way they were depicted in movies. There was only the pain and torment that was their constant companion each waking day. I heard their cries of fear. Jennifer, a sweet-faced woman with long, straight, brown hair, ran up and down the halls calling out for her mother. Someone said her mother had died several years back and she couldn't accept it so she ended up at the state hospital for months at a time. I wondered what it would be like to lose my mother to death. A fear settled in me, I pushed the thought to the back of my mind.

In the asylum, there were a number of old, two-story, brick buildings, ugly and aged with time. After a week,

Annie and I were considered sane enough to be sent to a cottage. It wasn't much better. After two days in the cottage, I made plans to run away when Gary came on Sunday.

"Are you nuts?" Annie asked. "If you get caught, you'll be sent to Cooper building. You know that."

Of course, I didn't plan to get caught. I just had to get away. It was out of fear, not bravery, that I was going to run—fear that I would become one of those women moaning in a relentless private hell. I knew what Cooper building was; the nurses made a point of letting us know we'd end up there if we didn't behave. Inside it was a huge room where patients slept on the floor with no beds, pillows or even sheets to cover themselves from the cold. Two toilets sat at either end of the room and the patients fought over who would use them first. Human waste was always present on the patients' clothing and on the floor. Those poor souls ate, slept and breathed in the confines of that filthy atmosphere. Attempting to run away was a mandatory thirty days in Cooper.

"It wouldn't matter," I told Annie. "I'd go crazy in there; I wouldn't know *where* I was."

On Sunday, I explained my plan to Gary, who loved me so much, he reluctantly agreed. I retrieved my cigarettes, then got into the car and Gary drove through the huge, iron gates without anyone even asking to see his visitor's pass. He was petrified. I was free! That evening, I called Mother. She spoke gently of her love for me and murmured, "My prayers have been heard." I cried like a baby.

But something had changed. There was a tone to Mother's voice, something perhaps she had not meant, nor was even aware of. It was pity. She did not ask me, though, how I was treated or what the asylum was like. That hurt me, though I would never have told her and caused her any more pain. I felt Mother was ashamed of me, and rightly so; I was ashamed of myself.

Only with age and wisdom would I be able to understand why she didn't ask. She already knew first-hand how horrible places like that are—from the one time Daddy allowed her to go with her brothers and sisters to see her own mama.

That night, Gary found me crying on our bed, our two sons, Monty and Shane, beside me. "Are you okay honey? You look weak. We love you. We'll take care of you."

After two weeks in the hospital, I was drained. I could see how a person could easily stay institutionalized for a lifetime.

NEW HABITS

After coming home from the state asylum, my body seemed to move in an almost lethargic manner, but my mind was abuzz with all kinds of awful thoughts. I began to picture horrible things Daddy had done when I was as a child, things I hadn't thought of in years.

Memories of the old mangy dog we had as children infiltrated my brain, thoughts of him haunted me. My mind revolved backwards and once again I lived those terrible days. On weekends, Daddy came home drunk. Half asleep, I could hear him curse as he walked up the rotten steps. I'd wake up and sit there in bed waiting for him to beat us. He'd always stop on the porch and try to pee on Old Joe, our dog, as he slept. I'd hear Daddy's zipper unzip and the urine stream down onto the dog as Daddy laughed and cursed. If Old Joe got up to run, Daddy'd kick him and tell him he wouldn't be fed for a week. Of course, I'd have burned in hell before I'd see that happen. We loved that old dog. I could hear him wailing and crying as Daddy kicked him. Even in the winter he'd run from his warm croaker sack on the porch to sleep in the field, because he was too afraid to return.

The only good ever served by Daddy's cruelty to animals was that it instilled in me a lifelong love for them and a fervor to fight for their rights. Old Joe is still as plain to me as that time so long ago.

It was about this time I first became obsessed with housecleaning. That obsession had not gone away. Now that I was married I worked feverishly for hours until everything was spotless and antiseptic like a hospital. I changed the linens on the beds twice a week which was fine, but the amount of hell that went into changing them was something I couldn't understand. The stripes on the sheets had to be perfectly lined on the bottom fitted sheet to match the top covering sheet, pillow cases were the same. Each side of the bed had to have an equal amount of sheet lapping over. Then came the corner tucks which were a nightmare because they had to be very tight and done in the military fashion. Panicky, I'd continue with the spread, shaking it in the air three times for any grit. It was never more or less than three times.

"One! Two! Three!" First I'd think it, then count it out loud. After nearly thirty minutes making the beds I was exhausted. Then it was time to wash the clothes.

Again all colors had to be put together after drying them. White towels were laid to another batch since they were mine. I only used white towels and wore nothing but white underwear. All stripes, plaids, or plain colors of linens were folded neatly, each exactly the same, and laid carefully in the linen closet. I took all bathroom things out for Gary and the boys. They were not allowed near my linen closet.

I made everything in my life more difficult and all things became rituals. Where other women used wax from a bottle, I had to have paste wax. I'd wax the hardwood floors on my hands and knees, smearing it with old towels, letting it stay on for one hour, no more, then buffing it with the electric machine until my image was reflected from every angle.

Rituals! All those damn rituals! I was wearing down my mind and body. The simplest thing became monumental and overwhelming. The irony of my mental illness was that I was almost always aware of what I was doing, I simply couldn't stop. I could not stop until whatever it was inside me had disappeared and run its course.

I would become totally frenzied, full of false energy that I exerted until I was exhausted. The key to the maze of my twisted mind was gone. I had lost all control, yet I performed my duties as a wife and mother and tried to let friends and family see only the parts of me that I wanted them to see.

However, there were things I couldn't hide from my husband and sons, like not being able to eat with them. I'd prepare dinner, set the table, put food on their plates and return to another room until they'd finished eating. At first I'd tell them I wasn't hungry. "I'll eat later," I'd say. But after a few months, they realized something was wrong with me. I had begun standing at the counter to take all my meals. This way, I could slide my plate further back and push my tea glass to the back of the counter. Also, since I was standing, I could walk away if I felt that familiar fear in my stomach. Fear of what? Of coming apart. Fear of losing control, throwing my plate full of food on the floor and smashing the glass against the icebox or the wall. Fear of shaking inside, of not knowing what caused it, and of running to the bathroom for refuge and security. I'd sit on the toilet, crying, praying Gary and the boys would just leave me alone until it passed. Sometimes I'd be so afraid I'd crouch in a corner of the bathroom and pull the clothes hamper in front of me, as if then I would be safe.

Then the attack would be gone. Afterward, I'd have chills; I'd take a scalding bath and be completely worn out. I could barely stand up, much less walk. My face would be white as marble, my speech low and moaning.

Almost everything I did was frenzied, every chore a hellish agony. The ritual of brushing my teeth is a good example of this behavior. First, I'd pack baking soda on to the wet brush and begin to scrub my gums, teeth, tongue. I had to be sure all residue was gone. This process took about fifteen minutes. Next, I'd spread toothpaste onto the brush and repeat the cycle, brushing my tongue until it was red; my gums ached and often bled. Then I'd gargle, inspect my mouth, bare my teeth in the mirror to see if there were any cigarette spots, and gargle again. Lastly, I'd rinse the brush until all paste was off the bristles and handle, placing it in its proper container beside the sink.

Afterward, the other terrors came. Washing my face was a major one. First, wet the face, then the cloth, then lather soap in my hands—not once or twice, but three times—and rub it vigorously on my face with only my hands, not the cloth. I'd rinse my face and then repeat the cycle. I'd wipe my face with a dry, clean hand towel after all the soap had been rinsed off, then with the wet cloth, then the towel again. Finally convinced I was now clean, I'd go about the rest of the housework.

I tried to make everything happen in periods of "threes." I turned faucets on and off three times, shook towels and most clothes three times while I was folding them, shook my arms by my side three times. Later I would become far more frenetic, when the "habits" were totally out of control and three times would not be enough to satisfy that urge in me.

One of my other habits soon grew more pronounced and embarrassing. I couldn't hide it from Gary and the children—I needed to smell everything. I smelled every bite of food that went in my mouth several times; I sniffed at the coffee and tea I drank. I smelled the food I cooked to satisfy myself it was fit for consumption. After I washed our dishes, I smelled each one. It was a nightmare from which I could find no escape and which I had no way of controlling.

Each piece of clothing was smelled not just once, but three times—sniff! sniff! sniff! Hanging them on the line—sniff again. But even that didn't cure the urge in me. They were smelled again when I dressed the boys, and often Shane would ask to smell it like his mama did. Gary's work clothes were laid out at night and yes, smelled. My own clothing was a never ending-nightmare.

Bra. Panties. Blouse or shirt. Pants or pedal pushers. I smelled each one right down to my shoes and socks. One obsessive habit in particular reduced me to tears. I loved white; it was my favorite color. I was always a roll-up-the-sleeves, turn-up-the-collar kind of woman. I felt like a movie star. Even my jeans had to be rolled up. I wore a man's white shirt, sleeves rolled high. Now, to get an even look on both legs of my jeans or both shirt sleeves required yet another ritual. I'd stand in front of the mirror, rolling up one leg, then the other. Then I'd turn around and see one was crooked, so I had to start again. I kept adjusting one, then the other to make it even. When the legs or sleeves would fold over the roll, I became so panicked I felt crazy. Up. Down. Fold. Smell. Crease. Smell. No end!

By nightfall each day I was exhausted and felt sick.

"Stop it. I don't like you like this," Mother said.

"Join the club, Mother. I don't like myself. Nobody likes me."

"Maybe I came at the wrong time of year. You haven't had enough time to recuperate from the—the mental hospital."

"And the sap's rising, right, Mother? No, it's dying this time a year. See, I am crazy! It's late November. Of course the sap's dying. Like you used to tell Daddy about Grandma Betty. She—"

"At times," Mama said slowly, "I see in you someone I never knew. And yes, my mama got worse every spring and every fall, without fail. Mama was insane, Jean. You're just sick."

I could feel my face turning pale. By the look from Mother, she saw it too.

"Why can't I be your little girl again, Mama? Why can't you love me like you did when you needed me? When we only had each other to comfort us?"

"Don't cry, honey." She reached out to touch my face and wiped the tears away. "Don't hurt yourself like this."

I walked outside to the porch and sat on the swing and let the crisp wind of autumn blow over me. As I sat there Mother came out and joined me. She held me in her arms like a small child. I cried and said, "I'm tired of hurting you and my family, tired of being sick."

"I'm so hollow and dead inside, Mother," I told her.

"Just cry. It'll do you good. And just let us love you. Don't push us away like we don't exist."

"I just can't seem to fit in with Mattie and the other girls. I don't really belong anywhere Mother, and I don't know how to live, how to let my family love me and accept their love. I just want to die, Mother."

She pulled me closer. "Hush. Don't say that."

"I know my love for you is much too possessive and unhealthy, but I can't help it. Sometimes I feel like I'm still in your womb and you'll always protect me and love me more than the others."

She held me off. "We have a special bond that will far outlast my lifetime. We've walked the coals of hell together. Perhaps because of it you're the saddest person I've known. I know something's wrong with you—I don't know what." She pointed to her head. "I know nothing about those things. But even as a child you were different. I felt you needed me as much as I did you. Some children need more nurturing than others."

I knew what she meant. My son Monty was like that. He clung to me like a barnacle to a pier, but Shane rode the waves, bounced with life and enjoyed living.

Not long after mother returned to New York, I received a letter from her saying that if I didn't get better she would not be able to come for another visit. She had talked with Dora and Beth and they felt her heart was at risk around me.

It was hard to accept the separation and say goodbye to Mama. Mama was the person I worshiped, adored, idolized, breathed for. She was the gentle woman who gave me life, the loving lady I clung to when Daddy was drunk and beating us. I put "Mama" in a safe place in my heart where I could take refuge and think of her. This other woman, the southern transport who lived in New York, was "Mother," and she had nothing in common with "Mama." Yet the longer I didn't hear from her or see her, the more fear I felt. I began to hate her.

8

ANOTHER GOODBYE

Though she was still young, Mother had suffered two heart attacks just months before my second son, Shane, was born. October of that year was when she moved to upstate New York to live with my sister Dora and her new husband. Something had begun to happen to my relationship with Mother long before she became ill, though. It became filled with a sharp, knifelike tension. Mother was like the closet to me; she was my security blanket. However, the day came when that feeling of false peacefulness abandoned my body. I realized I was dwelling in the past.

I'd have temper tantrums where I cursed like a sailor at the people I loved most. I was ashamed that I had become a bitch to live with. Each day brought on a new battle as I traveled my hellish road. I was tormenting myself, but couldn't help it. One day, after an argument in which I had wanted to talk about Daddy's death, Mother said angrily, "Look, he will never hurt you or me again. He's dead.

You'll have to grow up; I am cutting the cord. I love you, but you won't drive me crazy like you."

"I'm not crazy!" I pleaded. "I'm just sick!"

"Yes you are, honey. So—"

"Don't call me honey!" I shouted.

She was startled. "Why not?"

"Because you call everybody honey—your children, friends, grandsons, Gary—everybody. I'm not everybody, Mother, I'm your daughter. You and I have a bond—we will forever be *one*."

She shook her head in amazement. "That's sick, Jean! I'll try never to call you honey again. But we are not one person—you are a mother and wife—I'm not you, Jean. I love you—I will love you and pray for you as long as I live, but the past is over. Start living in the present."

"And you, Mother?" I asked, a half-smile curling my lips. "What about *your* past?"

She looked hard at me. "I put it where it belongs—in a tiny corner of my memory, never to be thought of again."

When she walked out, I flung myself across the bed and cried for hours. Then I grew angry. How could she say we were not as one? We had been together all the nights she needed me when Daddy was alive. That was the bond I felt between us.

How dare my own mother tell me to stop smothering and suffocating her! After all of our suffering together! I'd slept in the woods in the heat of summer and the cold of winter for her. I'd hidden with her in the potato patches with vines covering our bodies to escape Daddy's wrath. I had felt a snake crawl over my bare feet and dared not make a sound for fear Daddy'd find us. I had hovered near her frail body as we clung to each other and cried, hiding in a ditch, listening to him chase us. Rain and cold, no matter what the weather, we were as one. We slept together in the hayloft and prayed he didn't come there to feed the mules.

The sharecroppers who lived down the road also helped us. In the sweltering heat of August, we took refuge in their attic. Mama and I hid, bathed in sweat, eating only the sweet potatoes they passed up to us. For three days and nights, we'd hold our breath as Daddy would visit the house asking questions about us. After all that, she had forgotten? Fine. She could "cut the cord;" I'd play by her rules now. I tried to pretend it didn't hurt, but it broke my heart.

Despite these feelings, when she moved away I was flooded with relief. I couldn't understand it. Maybe she was right, maybe now I could grow up and be a real mother to my sons, a real wife to Gary and, just as importantly, a daughter she could love.

Yet, I was angry at her for leaving. When her letters arrived in the mailbox, I'd tear them into tiny pieces and burn them. I hated when she phoned. I knew I sounded phony and contrived, telling her how well I was doing with my therapist, making her believe I was still getting help.

Mother'd often ask me if I had a cold or wasn't feeling well. When I said I was fine she'd say that I sounded like a child who was sick. Other times she'd ask if I was angry because I sounded so angry. Realizing it was "Mama" I was talking to I'd quickly revert to my little girl voice and put her mind to rest.

The postpartum depression I'd been tormented with after Monty was born had lasted over five months. I was thankful I didn't have it with Shane.

When Shane was about two, long after Mother had moved, I began having some new kind of "attack." It first happened one day when Gary was driving me to the grocery store. We left our sons playing in the back yard with older children to watch them. It was only three blocks away, and we were halfway there when I broke out in a cold sweat. My head began pounding; it seemed to be on fire. I was petrified! "Gary, please stop the truck. If you don't stop, I'll jump out onto the highway in front of traffic."

"I can't stop. What's wrong, babe?

I begged him, but he was in the wrong lane. I wrung my hands and held on tight to the seat belt, wrapping it several times around my wrist so tightly it almost cut off my circulation. I shut my eyes tightly. After a few minutes he still couldn't stop, so I unbuckled the seat belt and crawled on the floor. I knew Gary was staring at me, but I wasn't really aware of anything except the horrifying fear that came out of nowhere. Finally, he pulled into the parking lot of the store.

"I'm here," Gary said softly. "Here, let me help you up."

"No! Don't touch me!" I shouted.

He was patient, as usual. He sat with me on the floor of the car until I was okay.

"You must be thinking how stupid I am, crawling on the floor, scared to death. I must be stupid!" I said.

"You'll be all right," Gary said gently as I walked inside the store with Gary holding my hand. We got a cart and started shopping. Helter-skelter, I threw cereal, Pop-tarts and everything else into the cart. That was not like me. Everything always had to be in its own place, in order. The aisles seemed wider, larger than ever. Space, empty or filled, became so overwhelming I felt like I had to scream. I felt foam forming in my mouth. I clasped my hand over my mouth and ran outside to the truck. I opened the door, got in and crouched down inside so no one could see me.

That night there was nothing else except the cold fear in my gut as I tried to act "normal" with Gary and the boys. I became overbearingly sweet and kind and even made myself sick. At my weakest, I desperately needed my husband and sons. I was a pathetic person. I hated myself for being so weak.

The only thing I could ever attach to the reason for that first "attack" was that Mother, who thought I was better, was coming for her yearly visit within days and I was scared to see her. I had one more "attack" after Mother arrived. I had met her plane, making sure to take her grandsons so they could talk with her. When we arrived back home, she and the boys got out of the car. I told her I'd bring in her luggage. A few minutes passed and she was already inside at the back door calling me, but I couldn't move. What in the name of God would I tell her? How could I tell her the truth when I didn't even know what the truth was? What was bringing on the attacks? So I lied. "I have to run to the store for ice cream," I called, and drove off. I parked on a side street and crumpled onto the seat, crying.

"Please, God!" I begged. "I'm so tired of being sick. I'm always sick. Let me be normal. I'd rather die than be afraid of my mama. I love Mama! Please, God!"

Finally, I went home. After supper, Mother and I washed the dishes while Monty and Shane asked her a zillion questions. After a while, I scooted them out and asked her about my three brothers.

"The boys are fine. They work for the railroad and take care of all my needs. In addition, I've my disability plus the small veterans check I receive because Daddy was in the Navy. All my medical bills are taken care of and what the boys don't get me, Dora, Beth and Mattie do."

"I know they take good care of you, Mother," I said. "I do all I can. They can see you anytime they chose. Beth lives nearby in the Bronx, Dora is just a mile or two from you and the boys are also there with you. Mattie has to follow her husband, being in the Navy, but they have money and she gets to see you often."

"I know, dear. What are you getting at?"

"Nothing really, Mother. I just don't think they realize that when I want to see you or you want to see your grandsons, Gary and I have to pay for round-trip plane tickets. Then I buy you all your cigarettes and clothes. I have two children, Mother, not one like your other daughters. I guess when they see us coming they say here comes Jean and her "herd."

"No, they don't." she said. "In two years, you've never been to New York to see me or your sisters. You have nothing to do with them; so they don't know you."

"Hell, I *don't* know them!" I turned to face her. "When I was in the state asylum I never heard one word from my sisters. In fact, I didn't even get a letter from you."

Our family discussion was finished. Not long after that, Mother left.

BREAKDOWN

One morning soon after Mother's visit, I drove to a shopping center to buy jeans for Gary and the boys. I came to a draw bridge as it opened to let a boat pass under it. My car was just two behind the stop bars. Suddenly, I began to sweat profusely. My palms became sticky, my breathing so rapid I could barely get enough air. I had an almost overpowering urge to jump from the car and throw myself into the black river below. Petrified, I took the belt from my jeans and tied it in knots around my left wrist, binding the other end around the steering wheel. I felt secure for a second: I couldn't jump into the river with my left hand bound to the wheel.

It seemed an eternity before the bridge closed and I slowly drove across. I knew I couldn't stand being in a store, so I turned back toward home a few blocks later. The closer I got to my own surroundings, the less fear I felt. Instead, I felt compelled to harm myself—to kill myself.

Once at the house, I managed to get out of the car. I

told myself I had to reach the front door, but the distance seemed far greater than the strength I had to walk there. Where was my watch? What time was it? I looked at my arm; it felt strangely disconnected. I reached the edge of the house and fumbled my way to the door. I turned the knob and I walked in, vision still blurry. Even so, I saw that the house was spotless. I must have spent hours cleaning to get it that way. The scent of pine cleaner filled the rooms. I must have mopped the kitchen and baths with it.

Every movement, every sound, even my own breathing seemed to be happening to someone else. It wasn't real. It was a dream. A nightmare.

As I looked around, the present scene faded. I saw Mama and Daddy and all of us children working on the farm. I seemed to be half in another world, moving between the farm and the present. Terrible scenes played in my mind.

Now I couldn't rid myself of the past. I ran through the house, searching wildly for the phone. I couldn't remember where it was and I had to call Gary. He'd know what to do. I was more than half crazy, I was convinced of that. Then I told myself I wasn't. Maybe I was going through an early change of life. Yes, that could be it. That was when Grandma Betty lost her mind. Oh yes, I kept telling myself. I will go peacefully insane and they'll carry me to the asylum just as they had Grandma—lock me up and I'll remain there the rest of my life. I'll be safe and I won't care if I'm in the insane asylum, because I'll be crazy and not even know it. I had it all figured out.

Chills began to wrack my thin, aching, trembling body. I was freezing. I made my way to the bathroom and pulled off my clothes. A hot bath! I always took a hot bath to get rid of the chills. I jumped into the tub, turning on only the hot water, having to feel my way since I was having difficulty focusing. I couldn't see a washcloth, so I grabbed for a towel and soaked it in the scalding water. I still had the sense to allow some cold water to come from the faucet, or I would surely have burned myself half to death. I lowered my body into the tub, immersing every inch of me except for my face and long blond hair. I lay there allowing the water to end the chills, hugging the soaked towel against my chest and neck.

I don't know how long I was there—over an hour, at least. Then, I got out and reached for a thick terry robe of Gary's. I didn't dry off, but pulled the robe on and found some warm slippers. I was so weak, I almost had to crawl to the living room. I curled up on the couch, throwing a blanket over my head. Then I shut my eyes, tight, so the fearful imagery wouldn't overwhelm me.

But I couldn't keep still. I jumped up and ran to the front door. I opened it quickly, then just as quickly slammed it and put the lock on. I was alone and safe. I lay back on the couch and pulled the blanket snugly around me, allowing its warmth to soothe my mind and body momentarily.I had my hands clasped over my eyes. As I peeped through my fingers, mad scenes from my childhood rushed by one after the other.

Panting harder and harder, I began to hyperventilate. No paper bag was within reach. I gasped, trying to draw fresh air into my mouth and slow my breathing down. I couldn't stop hyperventilating and had reached a panic-like stage as I made more futile attempts to take in air.

Somehow, I found the strength to run from the sofa to Gary's and my bedroom. I grabbed some blankets and crawled into the closet. There I crouched in the darkest corner and began screaming, crying and calling out for Mama. Over and over I called, but there was no answer.

It was then, almost subconsciously, that I reached up for a small box on the shelf in the closet. It was rat poison. We'd put it there out of reach of the children when we discovered we had a mouse problem.

I lay the box down and, getting a glass from the bathroom, filled it to the top with water. Back in the security and safety of my closet, I opened the box. Slowly, I began to eat the small pink pebbles, washing them down with the water. I ate till I couldn't swallow anymore. Then I put the box back on the shelf and lay on the floor, covering my trembling body with blankets. I slept for what seemed like only minutes.

Then, as if awakening from a nightmare just short of the point where I was about to be killed or fall from a building, I sat bolt upright and my eyes opened wide, staring into nothing. Lying back down again, I drifted into an unconscious state in which I was a child again and Mama was holding me. She lifted my lifeless body into her arms and carried me to the bed. She spoke words that were neither audible nor meaningful, but they were the sweetest sounds on earth. Her voice was like the gentle playing of a violin somewhere in the distance. She sang a song, the melody of which I couldn't recognize. Then she kissed away my tears and helped me up. Together we walked, mother and child, hand in hand, into a blissful void.

I didn't know at the time, but that peaceful oblivion was the first stage of the effects of the rat poison. Then something disturbed my tranquillity—I smelled death. I can tell you, its smell is like no other on earth. It is sickeningly sweet, like the nauseating aroma of rotting gardenias.

At some point, some semblance of rationality penetrated my stupor. I dressed, not wanting my boys to find me as I was when they arrived home from school. I put on a white blouse, purple corduroy jeans, cologne and brushed my long hair into two ponytails. I dabbed on some rouge and pink lip gloss to give me some color.

Then, I unlocked the front door, opened it and sat down in my rocker in the living room. I stared through the glass storm door as gray terns pranced gallantly about the yard. I was aware of putting my hands beneath me, sitting on them. And I waited. I waited for death.

CHAPTER

10

CHAIN MY BODY, FREE MY SOUL

Yet it didn't come. Monty and Shane got home from school and I was still sitting in the rocker. I talked to them, saying how much I loved and missed them each day. I sounded desperate to please, like a starved dog, and I hated myself for it.

Gary came home early because a bad rainstorm was about to flood Charleston. "I'm sick," I said, telling him nothing more. He looked searchingly at me. I could not hide the shaking or the nausea. "I'll be all right," I lied.

"Are you sure?"

Gary got two five-milligram doses of Valium from a friend and made me swallow them. Never having taken any drugs in my life, I quickly fell asleep and spent the weekend in bed sleeping or in the bathroom throwing up. My legs pained me so much I couldn't walk.

On Monday morning, I prepared breakfast for the boys while they got ready for school. Gary had already gone to work. A million crazy thoughts filled my mind, and when I could control them no longer, I ran to my bedroom. Quickly, I locked the door. I observed a hammer and nails in one of my hands and some tangerines in the other. I nailed the door shut. I didn't know if I was shutting myself in or shutting my precious family out. I heard the boys calling to me as they left, wanting to know if I was all right. The front door shut, locked and the bus drove away.

Later, I pried open the bedroom door back open. I ate the tangerines and smoked several packs of cigarettes. Then I took white sheets and draped them over all the mirrors in the house, drawing all the drapes and the blinds shut. I hid every knife and razor blade I could find, praying I would forget where I put them. The most vivid memory I have of that weekend is the intense pain into the bones of my legs. I'd never felt such agony. I kept it to myself and didn't tell Gary about the rat poison.

Days later, I checked myself into the hospital's psychiatric unit for nearly a month. During that time, not one nurse or doctor or so-called therapist knew what was wrong with me, except they agreed with my medical doctor and my gynecologist that I had suffered a complete and totally devastating breakdown. I was shot full of Thorazine, Stelazine and many other drugs, so I remained lethargic throughout my stay. My general physician, in consultation with my gynecologist, finally decided to release me into Gary's care, since they felt I was no danger to myself or others.

On orders from my doctors I went to visit a therapist. Alonia, a friend, was kind enough to allow her fifteen-year-old son Henry to stay home from school and drive me since I could no longer trust myself in a car alone. Henry was like a younger brother to Gary and often worked for Gary's construction company weekends. During my initial visit, the doctor, a thin, frizzy-haired woman in her fifties smiled at me countless times while drinking several mugs of coffee. She said little, just asked a few questions. I left feeling even greater desperation. Looking at her watch, she then dismissed me until the next week. The final visit was also my last straw. At one point, she accused me of having an affair with Henry. I was deeply offended, but my hurt quickly turned into anger.

"I didn't like you the first time I came here," I said, my mouth trembling as it always did when I couldn't control my anger. "But I didn't know you were such a bitch. Now I do." She showed me to the door in a rage. "I'm leaving!" I screamed.

"Good!" she snapped. "I certainly won't be treating *you*—"

I slammed the door in her face.

Later, I wondered if the whole world was screwed up. If not, was I the only person on earth who couldn't find a therapist who had the training and empathy to treat people like me?

For the next three months, my thoughts raced and fear dwelled in me constantly. I couldn't leave the house alone, couldn't drive the car and I functioned like a windup doll around the house. I grew more and more frantic about the housecleaning. I scrubbed the floors and walls till my knuckles bled, changed linens two to three times a week, washed the dishes over and over. I stayed alone and wanted nothing but peace. I was obsessed with death. I didn't think of death as being "final," but instead as the beginning of a life of peace.

Each day, I did frenzied things with my hands and body, but my mind's inertia was worse. It seemed to be painfully suspended somewhere between madness and sanity. Often I prayed for insanity to overcome me so I would just stop hurting.

The idea of having to talk to anyone other than Gary and the children caused me even more anguish. I'd see my neighbor in her yard and have to quickly close the kitchen blinds, even though I felt a great desire to run outside and confront her.

I was feeling so much anger towards human beings in general, but I'd see a stray dog in the yard and no matter how he appeared, plump or bony, I was convinced he was being abused and starved to death. I'd coax him into the yard and feed him. At one time, there were four or five strays taking refuge in my back yard.

Then there was a mind game I played. I called it "What if." What if I lost my mind? What if I harmed Monty or Shane? What if I killed myself? Daily life was intense; it was a never-ending battle with myself. It was destroying me as a person, wife and mother. The only time I felt normal was when I was "abnormal." Not long after the mind games began, I started seeing pictures of the Cooper River Bridge in my head. I had no greater fear than that I'd drive there and jump off it.

During this awful period, Gary was my only lifeline. He worked hard as a construction foreman to care for his family. Most of the time I wasn't even really his "wife" in the true sense. I loved Gary more than life. I could be across a room when Gary walked in and my heart would race like a schoolgirl in love for the first time. Butterflies danced in my stomach and I could almost taste the sweetness of his body against mine. That was when I had some semblance of sanity.

When I didn't, I hated the thought of sex. It became the most ugly and vulgar thing. Sex was nasty. I didn't want it. The mere thought of Gary reaching self-gratification through masturbation sent my mind reeling into a disturbing world of perverts and trashy people who had no values. They thrived like pigs wallowing in mud, crawling over each others' bodies and gorging themselves lustfully.

Three months had passed since that day on the lawn when I lost all reasoning—three of the longest months of my life. I was taking small amounts of Valium prescribed by my gynecologist, just enough to allow the exposed nerves of my mind to find peace momentarily.

And then Mother came. Yes, Mother, the lovely lady from upstate New York. Properly dressed, long nails red as beets, matching lipstick and clothes, skin so milky white it looked angelic. The only thing missing was her halo. Gary dearly loved my mother. She was gentle and kind, saintly. I hated that. She seemed to glide on air instead of trudging through the mud like us sinners. I couldn't pretend to be good like her.

It required years for me to deal with and accept the fact that I wasn't like Mother. In fact, nobody wanted me to be like her except me, and I hated myself for wanting that. I felt she was the perfect mother, the perfect woman, and I could not be perfect. I was human.

I tried desperately to be good. But, with her always before me as the model, I crumbled. After a while I was petrified to be around Mother. Her presence was overwhelming and filled me with fear. I was afraid I'd say the wrong thing, or she'd take something I said the wrong way.

If I voiced my thoughts, I thought she'd get upset and leave.

This time, she had been there just over three weeks and Gary had "fixed" me just as I had asked. I was chained by one hand to the rocker in which I sat in the living room, a blanket covering me. Then he took the boys out for hamburgers. They were gone when Mother got out of the shower. Still rubbing cream onto her delicate face, she entered the room.

"Can I get you something, Jean, before I sit down?" she asked. "Have you had your medicine?"

"Yes, Mother. Some fresh iced tea would be nice. There's plenty of snacks for you, " I called as she went to the kitchen. "Gary got strawberry ice cream and candy."

She brought us each a glass of tea and sat in Gary's recliner. The cream she had put on her face caused it to shine under the dim lamp and almost cast a glow around her, setting her apart from me, in a better world, as if she were God's creature and I were the Devil's. A pang of hatred filled me. I felt it burn in my guts and settle there like a bullet that could never be removed. Inoperable.

"You look tired, dear," she said. "Maybe you should lie down and rest. I'll be right here if you need anything."

"I know, Mother," I half whispered. "You always are. For everybody."

"What's that?"

"Nothing, Mother. Pay me no mind—*my* mind's nearly gone. It's been destroyed. I'm more than half crazy."

She lit a cigarette and inhaled deeply, blowing the smoke out slowly in small streams. Her long black hair draped about her shoulders and her mouth curled at the corners in a smile which I remembered from when she was

"Mama." She was indeed beautiful. She put her ruby-tipped nails on my shoulder and stroked it. I felt my own short bitten nails digging into the arm of the rocker.

"Would you like to talk?" she asked.

"Talk," I mumbled. "About what, Mother?"

"Anything. Whatever you want to. Anything."

"Anything? No matter what? The family? My sisters? You and me? Daddy's death? What about? Anything, Mother?"

She licked her bottom lip. That was the trait that never failed to take me back to my mama. "Anything, my dear," she leaned forward in the chair. "If it will really help you."

I didn't know if it would help or not but—"Daddy," I heard my voice say. "Can I talk about Daddy's death, Mother?"

She turned away. "I'd rather we wouldn't. Your sisters and brothers don't, and you shouldn't either."

"But there are things I need to know."

"Let the past die," she said.

"And what if I can't? What about me, Mother? I'm sitting here with a chain around my hand. Chained to this rocker." She rose quickly and came to me, inspecting my hand chained to the chair. "Don't, Mother! Put the blanket back over me. Don't look at this. I don't want to hurt you."

She was crying. Her delicate arms around me, cradling me like a lost child. "Why a chain, honey. Why, for God sake?"

"So I can't hurt anyone, Mother. Not you. Not the boys. Not Gary. Not even myself."

"Dear God. You could never hurt anyone. Not with your hands. You're too gentle for that."

I looked deep into her green eyes filled with tears. "I've hurt Gary, Mother. Sometimes I've beat on him with these little hands. Just like Daddy did to us."

"No," she shook her head. "Not you, honey."

"Yes, Mother," I cried. "I hate myself for it. Gary's such a good man—and I love him. But when he drinks too much beer, I go crazy—like a wild woman, Mother! I can't bear it."

Her face froze. "The man's your husband—not your child, for heaven's sake."

"Yes, just like Daddy was *your* husband—but he beat you every weekend like you were a child he hated and then he beat us children, too."

"I—just stop that! I hate when you talk about him, about those times. It's over; I won't let you bring it back."

"Mother, there is something else. After this nightmarish existence I've had to admit to myself I seem to have several personalities. They're all very different, and as I thought back, at least one began long ago in those days with Daddy. Gary says I'm so many different people, he never knows who he'll come home to find."

She stared at me. "I'm your mother. Don't you think I have sense enough to see you have personality changes? I see your moods—the way you change. Give me credit; I see it too."

I wondered if she saw at that moment the way my facial expressions were changing into those of little Jeanie, the child in me. I wondered if she noticed I was talking in that childlike voice from long ago, so sad and lost. Could she see and feel the pain in my eyes? My mind?

I began crying softly. I felt her gentle hands on my face as she wiped away the tears. In her eyes, I saw the pain she must have felt at seeing her daughter splintering, her hand wrapped in a chain attached to a rocker's arm. I was lost in a world of fear and bitterness. My heart ached, filled with love and sorrow for my mama. I lay my head against her shoulder when she reached across the chair.

"Cry, my little girl," she wept. "Cry, honey."

"Oh God, Mama! I love you so much! I wish I could accept that you're their mother, too. But I don't want to share you."

"You never have," she whispered. "I love each of my children in a different way—their own special way, the way they need nourishing. But you're so very special to me, because you need me in a special way. You need me for strength. You don't need that chain around your arms. I could never be afraid of you."

"Look at the chain, Mama," I cried. "See. It's not locked. It's only in my mind. It makes me safe, feel safe. But it's not locked."

"It never was?"

"No, Mother. It's the boys' bicycle chain. They lost the lock and key."

Mother sighed. "You know, I'm not a very intelligent woman. I maybe wise at times but you're so gifted, my child. You have a wonderful imagination like a small child's. In a way, you're more lucky than you realize. Not many of us remember how it was to think and feel like a child, the pure joy of it."

"And the pain, too, Mother," I said. "All the torment."

She didn't reply. I longed to talk with her about the things that caused me deep hurt, and yet I didn't want to make her life painful for her again. We'd taken too many beatings together. No, I could not rip open the old wounds and make them bleed again. My love for her was far too strong. But the murderous memories which remained in my thoughts were so agonizing, they caused me physical sickness. And buried beneath them was an even more nameless terror whose dimensions I felt but didn't yet know.

I started telling Mother about how obsessed I was about my housework and other things. How I changed around the furniture at least twice a week, how I was compelled to make the beds over and over till all the lint was gone. If the boys sat on my bed I'd have to repeat the process.

"You had that habit as a child, Jean," she said. "When I washed clothes, I had to try and get all the lint off yours. If I didn't, you'd pick at the material till it was full of holes. I had to sew them, hide them or throw them away to keep your daddy from finding them. You were different then, my child, and you're different now. Special. Like a child of God. To harm you is to harm a child. I knew I'd always have to be careful with you, with what I said and did. Love you more—no, not more, different. You needed me differently than the others."

"The weakest link in the chain," I told her. "Why must I always be in the eye of the storm, in limbo, never knowing who or what I am? Why can't I be normal? Normal like your other children?" I sighed. "I just want to die."

"No, dear," she said. "Death is final. Peace is not. I believe one day you *will* get help. A good, decent doctor with knowledge about these things will help you. I hope it's soon. I have to believe that, honey. There *is* help out there, and so long as there's hope, you'll survive. Because you're strong—a fighter, not a quitter. You'll beat this demon. And that I know is fact. You will win."

"Then I have a long way to go, don't I?" I asked. "I can't go hide in closets, eat rat poison and hope to get well, can I, Mother?" She moaned in shock. I clasped my hand over my mouth. "Oh, God! I'm sorry, Mother. Oh, please forgive me. I forgot. I made Gary promise not to tell you—please, Mother."

She tried to say something, but her voice trembled. I saw that look in her eyes, the look that questioned my sanity. To try to take my own life, to harm my body, which was God's temple—to put rat poison inside me, this act was one she couldn't comprehend.

Mother would be leaving soon to go back. A part of me was so relieved and a part ached for her love and companionship. On the day she was flying home, we cooked dinner together and tried to fill the void between us.

"Do you ever think of that night?" I asked her as I fried some chicken for Gary's and her favorite recipe. Then I thought—you idiot! Why did you ask that? She'll be mad. She'll fuss at me. Stupid me.

Never looking at me she said, "Only when I'm with you, dear. I reckon I'll always think about it when I'm with you, but I don't want to dwell on it. We'll take the secret to our graves with us. Right?"

I looked at her strangely, puzzled.

My back was to her. I wondered if she could see that I was shaking as I tried to hold back the tears. "Right, Mother. We'll never share it with anyone."

"Especially your brother Robert, Jean. Promise me."

"I promise."

"*Especially* not to Robert, never."

She was so close to me, I felt her breathing against my neck. Her hand came slowly to my face and softly smoothed back a strand of hair. I knew she was waiting for my answer. I turned and looked at her beautiful face and I sensed a smile curling on my lips.

"No, Mother. Never. Especially not Robert."

But to myself I thought, how can I talk about things I don't understand? I wanted to have a new secret now, only her and me, so once again we would become allies. I won't talk to him, Mother. I'll just stand back and watch my brother go totally insane like me, but I'll never betray your trust, dear Mother.

CHAPTER
11

ADDICTION AND
PANIC ATTACKS

During the next few years I got sicker and sicker. I was in and out of mental hospitals and psychiatric wards. I became a walking image of what ended up in such places. They were institutions which robbed you of any of your self-respect, dignity, motivation to live and willingness to get better.

I attempted suicide countless times and seemed to be on a fast track to self-destruction. In a way, I counted on "death" to save me. Death was my friend and my constant companion, yet nothing I tried would kill me. Seventy-seven yellow Valium and all I did was sleep for a few days. Cutting my wrist with a razor blade, I watched it bleed, knowing I would surely find my peace. Not wanting to see all the blood, I draped a towel around my wrist and lay down. Of course, I believed as I lay on the bed I would lose so much blood I'd go to sleep and never awaken. But death eluded me and so did peace and sanity.

Elevil, Melaril, Tofrinil, Atavan, Vistril, Nardil, Stelazine, more Thorazine, Valium, Valium, and more Valium, Librium, Xanax. Doctors gave me all of them. Nothing worked. For a while I was totally addicted to yellow Valium. My world was one of torment and pain.

My sons were growing up. I was missing all the joys of being a part of their lives.

The irony of my mental illness and the treatments which didn't work was that I functioned as a wife and mother most of the time, keeping those awful secrets about compulsive behavior to myself. Sometimes doctors saw me when I was sane and good. Then I'd cry endlessly, becoming a childlike person they all pitied. On other days I was a "bitch," showing another side of my warped mind. But in the end, all these personalities were brutal and destructive.

I was becoming more confused and even sicker. My sickness was catching up with me. I'd be in therapy, maybe thinking I was getting better, and I'd feel myself losing touch with reality. Disoriented, I'd forget who and what I was. Had I been the little lost child, the "bitch" or the good wife and mother? Or was I a distorted blend of the three? I'd become frantic, rubbing my face so vigorously it would become red and my body would shake without control.

"Stop, you're torturing yourself," the therapist would say. "Just let us help you. The burden is too much for you."

She was right. I was killing myself and had no knowledge of how to stop. The once beautiful marriage I shared with Gary was now a nightmare. The boys constantly heard our arguments, ones that I always started for reasons I never understood. When I was normal, Gary worshiped me, adored my gaiety. But when I became the "others" he didn't understand, he hated me and started drinking. The stranger I got, the more he hated the situation and the more he hated it, the stranger I became. It was a vicious cycle. He drank more, grew angrier and I'd lose control completely.

So Gary drank, and I was crazy. What came first, the chicken or the egg? I was sick long before I met this wonderful man and fell deeply in love with him, and he drank long before he met me. Perhaps we aggravated our own frailties. He'd curse me for the day I was born, and the next instant hold my trembling and crying body against him, murmuring he loved me. I'd feel safe for a while.

My horrible obsession with cleaning and organization was eating my mind alive. An ashtray out of place was a disaster. I had awful attacks if I found the closets in disarray. All hangers had to face the same direction, hooks had to face the wall. All clothes colors had to be hung together; whites all in a perfect row, blues the same, etc. Shirts hung together, pants together; everything had its place.

I constantly straightened Monty and Shane's dresser drawers because of my obsession. They were my sons, the very blood of my soul and my love for Gary, so nothing could be out of place for them. Their room had to be perfect. The toys in their room always had a freakish appearance—as if they were on display, waiting for inspection from some mean military woman. The moment they put a toy down, I grabbed it and put it in their toy box. I dusted and polished toy soldiers and musical boxes with strings, wiped out the window sills around their beds every day and changed their linens for them twice a week or more if a "spot" appeared.

They could open their dresser drawers in the night

and take out exactly what they wanted. Socks, T-shirts, shorts and night clothes all neatly—no, perfectly—stacked in rows in the drawers. Different patterns or stripes or flowers had to be lined together as if a flower would spoil a stripe and render it worthless. Their clothes were laid out on the spotless beds every night after they bathed. I hated for them to open the drawers. I panicked if I saw a dresser drawer even partly open. I could not calm down again until I had closed it and touched all the drawer knobs with my fingers. My hands or fingers had to make contact with the knobs, as if by so doing I was securing them from being opened again.

Often, I would scream at the boys because of things left out of place. Then out of the shame felt, I'd hug and kiss them, scoot them into the television area, and work frantically on undoing any "damage" they'd caused. Of course, this great and monumental damage was probably nothing more than a toy out of place.

I didn't exist any more. Someone had invaded my body, mind and soul. I lived in a frenzied world of picking up lint, trying to kill myself with any pill or weapon I could find. I was in and out of mental hospitals several times a year until nothing seemed real or normal except insanity. I was a walking stick of dynamite, ready to explode without warning.

"Be careful around her," people seemed to be saying. "She's mentally ill. Pay attention to what you say to her. You know her mind. Gotta watch what we say and do around her. She can't help it; she's just crazy!"

That seemed to be the rule of thumb except with my brother Robert, who walked the same road I did. I saw my other brothers and sisters only once every few years. One time they all got together at a motel, all except Mother due to her failing heart. They came to Charleston from all over the country to have a reunion. I later saw pictures and it seemed complete. All the children were in it, except me. I had no place in the picture; I didn't belong there. I didn't know these people, and I didn't want to know them. I knew my little brothers and sisters on the farm; they were my family, not these strangers in the picture. These new people frightened me.

I hadn't seen Mother since my breakdown. We spoke by phone sparingly, strained and tense. We wrote letters that were more like notes to a friend you weren't quite sure was still your friend. One day I decided to write a long letter. I told her mostly about Gary and the boys. Monty was fifteen now, tall and handsome and olive-skinned like his father. Yet, he was very easily hurt like me.

My baby Shane was no longer a baby except in my eyes. He was twelve. Shane's hair was blond like mine, his skin white and milky like mine and he hated to be told he looked like me. To him, that was "queerish." The boys played ball all the time. Any kind of ball. Gary was always on the field coaching either them or another team. I knew Mother would love hearing about the boys, but in the last paragraph of my letter I had something else to say, something that plagued my heart and hurt me.

"Mother," I wrote. "I pray you will not take offense, but Robert is very sick. He lives in a world of lies. He's asked me about the night of father's death. He imagines things. He thinks he's going crazy! Please, Mother. Won't you talk about it?" I closed it with all the love I had for my beautiful, precious Mother, signing it with kisses.

Her reply never mentioned Robert. Not a word.

I tore it into shreds and flushed it down the toilet. That fear of the "Mother" who was not my mama settled into my guts. My stomach churned and I shook. I'd never be free of that fear of this new woman. But why, God? Why did I fear my mother?

After my rebuffed letter, I became even more depressed. I functioned like a wind-up doll, performing my wifely and motherly duties as involuntarily as the blinking of my eyes. I did them, but did not comprehend them.

Then one dark, dreary morning, the sun had no color. There seemed no reason to get out of bed, to breathe, to put one foot before the other on the floor except maybe for a cup of coffee. The pain and fear became so great, I couldn't imagine living through that day. I was sure I would lose my mind completely. Death was the only answer. It was the most peaceful thought I had. All-consuming, I was obsessed with this thing we call "death," the finish, the end.

It was early November. The sap was dying in the trees. I hated this time of year. Nothing was alive. Yet fall was usually Monty's and my favorite time of year. As I watched the scene, I realized it was a day not unlike that one almost five years back, that wretched day I had a breakdown. Once again, I though of Grandma Betty, the sinking sap and how she got worse at that time of year. I could see her old, timeless, wrinkled face, see the emptiness in her eyes that seemed dead. Her face seemed to be everywhere I looked in the house.

I walked to a nearby grocery store, watching the movements of the faceless people. I found the item I wanted, went to the checkout counter, paid for them and walked back outside. I was surprised that my legs moved as I walked; I wondered if they were moving through some supernatural energy of mine, since I was not aware of expending any of my own. I took a cigarette from the pack in my pocketbook, put it in my mouth, lit it, then aimlessly inched my way homeward.

I lay the pack of cigarettes on the table, on which were also a large ashtray and lighter. Beside it was a large bar of Baby Ruth candy and the brown package I'd purchased. I opened the candy, threw the paper on the table and began slicing down the center of the bar. I spread it open like a hot dog bun pressing it down on both sides.

Next, I opened the box and took out the pinkish-brown rat poison that was packaged in small hunks. I pressed the poison down into the center of the candy bar in the opening I'd cut filling it in. Quickly, I rewrapped my potion and lay it carefully on the bare table, as if it were either dynamite or a precious jewel that I had to protect. Then I fixed a large glass of iced-tea, sat back down at the table, lighting another cigarette and inhaling deeply.

Putting out my cigarette butt in the ashtray, I slowly began to eat, taking small bites at first, washing it down with tea. The poison had no taste, just the sweetness of the candy. I swallowed hard, wanting to hear it plunge down my esophagus, propel itself into my stomach and begin to do exactly what it had said on the box. "FATAL IF SWALLOWED." This time I would not settle for anything less than death. With the final bite consumed, I read the label again.

I repeated it over and over in my mind. Fatal. Fatal! Did that not mean I would die? Gary wouldn't be home for several hours. I had given the boys permission to play at a friend's house that evening. Even if they came back home, they'd think I was taking a nap, not disturb me and go about their playing. I was safe. I locked my bedroom door, never wanting it to be my sons who found my dead body. I knew when I didn't open the door, they'd call Gary at work. He'd come home and take care of things. Gary always took care of things, didn't he? He never let me down. Once they found out I was dead, they'd cry and long for me. I'd lie in a rented casket for an hour to allow my sons to see that I was dead and then my family would have me cremated, according to my instructions. Later they'd scatter my ashes in the yard where Daddy and Mama lived and he died.

I lay on my bed smoking and waiting for the poison to flow through my body and drain the life from my useless being. My destructive, horrible soul. Images danced in my mind of countless football games with Monty the quarterback, skinny Shane the wide receiver and Gary the coach. Good times with the three men I cherished.

And I thought of time. What was this cruel thing, time? I couldn't see it, couldn't touch it, couldn't hold it in my palm and shape it. I remembered being twenty, when I couldn't imagine being any older—young and beautiful forever and time was good to me. When I was thirty, it was unthinkable that I'd ever become older—in the prime of my womanly beauty and sexuality, lips full and hope in my eyes. Now I was thirty-five and no, life could not go on any longer for me. Time was hell. I just wanted it to stand still until I took my final breath and found peace. Instead, I fell head first into more waking nightmares.

12

PAINFUL IMAGES

Slaps. Kicks. The belt zooming in the air. Faces in a circle. The long, narrow kitchen. Cries of pleading, begging. Mama, Mama! My dear Mama!

We marched around the long wooden table, slowly, then hurriedly to avoid the belt. The leather made a slapping sound as it whipped back, doubled and cracked in the air. After taking so many licks, as we marched around the table like good little soldiers, I became numb.

I was dancing around, barefoot, a million little pieces of glass under my feet. As they pierced the skin, I felt a stinging sensation. Looking down, I saw blood everywhere. It gushed from many places on the soles of my feet. Blood mixed with glass. I shuddered; I hated glass. It petrified me. Then the belt struck again. Mama was watching it closely, trying to see how fast she should walk in order to take our licks for us. It was like musical chairs, except Daddy used a doubled leather belt or, sometimes, two belts plaited like a child's hair. He saw what Mama was doing, trying to protect me and Dora and Mattie. Daddy slapped her hard and made sure we got our own licks. When he finished, he laughed to himself in a soft, self-satisfied way. He was proud of keeping "his girls" in line.

The cabbage had set him off that night. I'd asked for a second helping of cabbage and it had angered him because his sister and her family were there for Sunday dinner. He'd cursed and ranted until they drove off. Then he threw our drinking glasses to the floor. When enough had been shattered, he got the belt and his sick game of "ring around the table" had begun.

Mama was holding me now, kissing my welts, speaking words of love to us girls. She rubbed salve and Vaseline on our small bodies saying determinedly, "I will outlive him an' show you children there is good in the world."

This scene faded, but others took its place. In the next one, hoe handles drew back and struck me and Dora for not getting all the weeds out of the cotton field, or being careless and chopping down a hill of tobacco by mistake, digging a shallow hole and covering the severed leaves with dirt. But he found out. He always did. And the hoe came crashing down against our backs, wails of terror sounding through the field as we hollered for mercy.

Then the cabbage was back in my mind. A huge bowl full of it was sitting in front of me. How many bowls had I eaten? He was screaming and cursing for me to eat more. "Eat it all!" he yelled. I began choking as he spoon-fed more and more to me, not giving me time to swallow before thrusting a glass of tea to my mouth.

Suddenly, I felt something warm spreading between my legs; I had wet myself. Although he was still force-feeding me, it now seemed like it was happening to someone else. Yet I could still feel the food being crammed down my throat, burning my mouth, and hear the gagging sounds I was making. At some point, I drifted into a peaceful state—like dozing off for a short nap, one that carries you into an unreal world where nothing touches you.

As this scene vanished, still another appeared. In and out of reality I drifted. Mama's belly was swollen with Will, her second son. I saw her sitting at Daddy's feet, taking off his boots. His foot was pressed against her buttocks. As she pulled, he pushed. The boot popped off. With the same motions, they loosened the other one, too. Then, as Mama turned to take off his shirt, his foot shot upward and hit Mama hard in the abdomen. He kicked her twice before she could get away.

"My baby! My unborn baby!" Mama cried, reeling backward. "Oh, God!"

"Baby! Baby, my asshole!" he grinned crazily. "Pregnant in the summer, barefoot in the winter. It's all women want."

Another picture intruded on this sick scene. A hot Sunday afternoon. Mama napping in bed while he was off with his "whores." When he came back, he entered the room, while his friends waited outside, and slapped her face over and over with a folded magazine. When I could bear it no longer, I ran to the kitchen and crawled under the table. No, I thought, he'd find me here. I inched across the splintered floor and got inside the pantry, hiding behind a fifty-pound sack of flour. I heard his laughter in the yard as he kissed those women and told his "buddies" goodbye.

Soon after this incident, Mama's baby was born ill. She protected her pale, sickly son fiercely the rest of her life. Will suffered from some sort of breathing problem; they took him to several doctors, but he was never diagnosed. If he got angry or started crying, his face would turn blue and he'd hold his breath. I think Mama always wondered if Daddy kicking her stomach had hurt her child.

Maybe the poison was working on my brain. I faded in and out of reality; the scenes from my childhood seemed *so* real. I took too many Elavil once and had hallucinated. I'd seen giant, black, spotted snakes crawling on the floor and over my body. That's what the poison was doing, I thought—taking away my brain, devouring my mind from the inside out.

A short time after little Will was born, Grandmama Adda was killed while driving home with her sister's husband after shopping in town. My great uncle was in a big hurry to get home because he drove our school bus. They were thrown from the vehicle and both died on the road, lying covered in the blood and raw rice that spilled during the wreck.

Drunk even at his mother's funeral service, Daddy took out his anger and hurt on us. It was our fault Grandma Adda died because we had never liked her, according to him. Grandma lay ever so still in her casket. In the air, there was an indescribable smell of death that sickened me. Pounds of paint and rouge were plastered onto her old face. Her eyes were wide open and seemed to be staring at me. My breathing grew rapid.

Then, still through the haze of memory, I realized it was not actually her lying in the casket. I was seeing that awful, oval-shaped picture of her that hung on our sitting room wall over the sofa. The sole possession Daddy had wanted to inherit, it had brownish, coffee-like stains around the white-rimmed paper, and I thought it must have been taken a hundred years ago. In it, she appeared as ghostly as she did in the casket.

The images changed again. The sound of khaki rubbing against khaki filled my ears. Daddy wove in and out of sight, running through the tobacco field. She was giggling like a school girl. I wanted to run, hug Mama's skirt and tell her—but I couldn't move. I hid, curled up in a ball behind the tall plants as she came closer. He was chasing a pretty, honey-skinned woman, younger than Mama, with the biggest brown eyes. She was a mulatto hired hand down for the summer to work tobacco. Daddy's naked back was tanned from the sun and was nearly as brown as hers. He reached her, she let him catch her and they kissed, lying between two rows. I caught glimpses of their naked bodies, sweaty and glistening in the noonday heat of August. Frozen, I was glued to the sounds of lust which filled my ears. When they had finished, I watched Daddy standing naked, trying to put on his pants while her hands touched him everywhere, but mostly on his groin. I felt sick to my stomach.

There was a peculiar odor about him when he came up to the house for dinner. Mama smelled it. She said something, and he grabbed her hair and dragged her, crying, from the kitchen to their bed. As they passed me, I could see that her face was red from being beaten. He marched her back into the kitchen minutes later, after he had taken her like a beast. He slapped her tiny behind and spoke with a twisted grin on his lips, "Now get dinner on the table, Sara pet. Gotta get back to the fields. Ain't no reason you bein' mad now, woman. I give you the same thing I give that gal. Only thing was, she appreciated it more. Get a move on, woman."

After he left I went to Mama.

"Hateful Daddy! Make him die, Mama!"

"No," she scolded. "It's a sin to wish him dead. He'll die soon enough. God will see to that. You understand?"

No! No! I don't, I screamed inside. I hate him! Die! Die!

Now the mental pictures of my tormented childhood began to mix with thoughts of Gary and the boys. Was I dead? Sleeping? In some kind of coma? Unconscious? Perhaps I was drifting into a place where only sick minds like mine can go. A place we go submissively, quietly, without protest, almost as if we are being escorted into a peaceful refuge within the torment.

Once again I saw my childhood. This time I was running, faster and faster, but my feet could not move. They were fighting as we walked along a country road. I was screaming to Mama, "Run, Mama! Run faster! Don't let'm catch you! A car's coming. Get off the road, Mama!" I saw him gripping her fragile body against him and nodding "morning" to the car's passengers. When it was out of sight, he released his fierce hold and she crumpled to the ground.

"Your ribs, Mama? I know he broke'em. Are they all broke, Mama? Will they heal back? Ever? Yessum, Mama. I'll wrap the cloth 'round'em. Will that make'em well, Mama? Will it?"

Suddenly this scene disappeared and bright lights were burning through my closed eyelids. As my eyes opened I saw people standing around me. Was I dead or dying and going toward the long tunnel of light people spoke of who'd come back from the dead? If I was, I sure didn't like the light. There was nothing warm and comforting about it. It wasn't soothing me and beckoning me to "cross over." Male and female voices were all around me. Somewhere in the distance I thought I heard Shane shouting. A black substance gushed from my mouth like an oil well. It flowed over my chest, soaking me. I knew it was going to choke me. It stuck in my throat, and gushed forth even more. What was it? I screamed for help but no one answered. Why couldn't they see I was choking? Why couldn't they hear me?

My stomach was hollow like an empty barrel. My body ached, throbbed and there was an intense burning sensation between my legs. I felt my hand move down and try to tug something out of my vaginal region. A strong hand stopped me.

"Don't do that!" a feminine voice called out. "If you pull it out, you'll rip your kidneys to pieces." My hand kept searching for the tube inside me. "Strap her hands down. If she doesn't die from the poison, she will from the damage to her kidneys. Strap them. Quick. And put the wraps around her stomach and chest. Hurry."

"Charcoal's getting a lot of it out, doctor," another voice said. "Hurry with the wraps, nurses. She's got a helluva lot of strength for a tiny woman eat up with rat poison."

"At least we managed to get *that* from her." Gary said. I tried hard to say something coherent. He was beside me, listening to me mumbling and trying to figure it out. "Please, Jean!" he urged. "Tell the doctors what it was. What was the name of the poison? They have to know."

Then Monty's voice rang in my ear. "Mama! I love you. You can't die! Tell us what you did with the box.

Don't die!"

"I don't care anymore," said Shane. His words cut into my foggy mind like a razor. "I don't care if she dies. I don't care." He was crying.

"Shut up, Shane!" Monty shouted.

"Boys! Please, don't!" Gary said.

"What can you expect, Mr. Brinson?" a woman asked. "These boys have lived a lifetime of being in emergency rooms watching us pump out their mother's stomach, trying our damndest to keep her alive when all she wants to do is die. Maybe we should walk away and let her die. I would, except my Hippocratic oath prevents it."

"You're a doctor, for God's sake!" Gary said. "You have to keep her alive."

"That will take a miracle, Mr. Brinson! If she lives—"

"What do you mean, *if*? Mama *will* live. She has to!"

"We hope so, Monty, for your sake. But—"

"Tell us," Gary said desperately. "Will she make it?"

"There's not a doctor in this room who'd say yes to that. Even If she does survive, Mr. Brinson, she's abused her body for years. She may be a beautiful young woman, but inside she's old. She wants to die. Go home, Mr. Brinson. Take the boys. Look for the box. If we find out the ingredients, we might stand a better chance of counteracting them. Without that, there's only a slim hope."

"Desk!" I heard myself mumble, barely audible. "My right—desk drawer."

"Let's go, Daddy! She said her desk drawer where she writes. Hurry, Daddy!"

Somewhere within the tormented confines of my mind, I heard this tiny voice, like a little girl, saying something strange.

"It's not their mama you want to kill, Jean. It's me! It's Jeanie Small."

And I could see that child—skinny, ragged Jeanie Small, cowering in a closet. This was my last image before I fell asleep again.

13

THROUGH THEIR EYES

That first time I'd taken the poison, my stomach was never pumped; instead, I ate or drank raw eggs and puked my guts out. But not this time. This was a strong poison, and it was in my small, frail body for over five or six hours before I was taken to the hospital by ambulance after Gary found me. My pulse had been so faint no one could find it.

Try as I might, I could not get out of bed. In my legs, I felt an excruciating pain I'd never felt before. Even the weight of the thin, white, ribbed spread someone had thrown over me seemed to crush them.

I looked around at my surroundings. A nice, private room with one bed. There were sheets on the mattress, a night stand, a mirror on a door (unbreakable, I was sure) and there were no bars anywhere. No, I wasn't back at the state asylum in Columbia. This was just another of the countless hospitals I'd been in for treatment. This time, it was the psychiatric hospital in Charleston.

A woman entered the room. She was a strapping woman, more muscular than fat. At times she operated like a military nurse commanding her fallen soldiers. She dressed not in white clothing like a doctor or nurse, but in street clothes. Never letting her eyes meet mine, she walked over to my bed, took my hand and recorded my vital signs.

"How do you feel, Jean? Weak?" she asked, staring straight ahead.

"Yes," I nodded, licking my dry lips. "My legs! What's wrong with my legs?" My voice was hoarse.

"Oh, *that*!" she said sarcastically. "That's the rat poison you eat for a regular diet. It's eating the calcium right off your bones—especially the legs. You know, Jean, like acid?"

Oh, God. Oh, God, I thought. "How long have I—?"

"You were in intensive care two days and nights. And you've been up here a day. Know where you are?"

"Yes," I nodded again. "Am I committed? Did Gary commit me?"

"No, Jean. We thought we'd just let you stay here till you get well enough to go out and eat some more poison. Then your poor family can rush you to ER and they can pump out your stomach again. I mean, we really enjoy your little trips here, Jean. It breaks the monotony of every day, ordinary insane people."

"I take it I'm committed?"

"Good guess." She wrote on her chart. "You'll start therapy for your legs today even if you have to crawl, which you likely will at first."

"Who are you? Why are you dressed that way?"

"We all wear regular clothes like the patients so we'll

blend in and not frighten them. I f we're lucky, they'll think we're one of them and not try to kill us. I'm a psychiatric RN. I give you your meds on my shift, have meetings with you and your family—I'm available if you want to talk. I try to get inside your brain and see what makes you want to die. My name is Ann Avery. Call me Ann. We're not very formal here."

"You don't like me, do you?" I asked.

"It doesn't matter if I like you, Jean. Do you like yourself? Apparently not. Look," she leaned over the bed and pulled the covers around me. "I'm not a bitch. I just had a bad morning—and night. My husband came home from work at 1 A.M. and wanted sex. The baby cried all night. Teething. And I need to lose twenty pounds to fit into a size twelve."

I tried to smile. "I understand."

"No, you don't, Jean. You try to kill yourself, and people care for you 'round the clock. I try to be a good wife and mother and the best damn RN. I can be. But nobody cares enough about me to say thanks or ask how I feel today."

"I'm really sorry you have to care for me, Ann. I—"

"It's my job. And I'll do a damn decent job if you let me. We've been giving you Demoral every three hours for the pain. We wanted to start with morphine, but our superior, Dr. James, wouldn't allow it. Said it might cause you to get confused or hallucinate. We've been feeding you Enfamil, baby milk, with IV's. Today you start drinking it from the can, eight to ten cans a day. More if you can stand it."

"What for?" I asked.

"To try and replace some of the calcium the poison is

eating away. Your meds are the pain killer plus fifteen milligrams of Valium a day." She paused and then went on. "There are rules here, as you should know by now, Jean. We don't wear nightclothes to walk down the hall, since we have both men and women here. No smoking except in the day room. No phone calls except during the hours listed on the blackboard. It says, 'calls permitted 10 A.M. till 11 A.M. and 2:30 P.M. till 3:30 P.M.' All eating will be done in the kitchen; you can have drinks in the day room."

I didn't care about those stupid rules. "Where's Gary? Where's my family?"

"Mr. Brinson and your son, Monty, have sat by your side many hours up here. And I hear they stayed outside the ICU room till the doctors said you would live."

"And Shane?"

"He stays in the day room. Refuses to come to your room. He's a very angry young boy right now. He loves you a lot, Jean, and he's hurting." She started to leave and turned back. She stared at me, then and changed the subject. "Look, someone will be coming for you in a few minutes. They'll help you get a bath and eat what you can; make sure you drink the Enfamil, Jean. I'll be back in an hour to start therapy with you for your legs."

"What will we be doing?"

"Walking, Jean. Just trying to walk up and down the corridors. Around and around in a circle. If you can't walk, then you'll crawl. Then walking. Then jogging. Whatever it takes."

How sad. How childlike. How lost. Nobody was saying those things to me this time. Nobody cared. I had tried to kill myself too many times, and even the doctors and nurses didn't care if I died. Well I'd show them. I was a survivor! I must have been. With the amount of rat poison I'd eaten, the doctors said a strapping horse couldn't survive. Gary had found the box in my desk. It was guaranteed to be fatal if swallowed by human beings.

I was very weak. Ann and I began inching our way down the long halls. Even if I fell on the floor, no patient or staff member was allowed to help me up. I was on my own, do or die or crawl and beg. Well I would not stoop to begging! After all, R.J. Small was dead and I had never stooped to begging since the day he took his final breath. Why would I start now?

I dragged my aching legs along. I cursed the day I was born. I cursed God for allowing me to survive rat poison and all the other things I'd tried. My anger toward God, partially composed of fear, convinced me I would burn in hell if I ever did manage to die. I cursed the doctors for keeping me alive. I cursed Gary and the boys for taking matters into their own hands, for playing God to save me. But the doctors assured me and Gary that it wasn't they who'd saved me. What saved my life was not known to medical society. They had no answers. Everything they had learned in years of medical school defied what I had lived through.

I recalled Mother telling me that her daddy, Papa Jim, was a drunkard till age thirty-seven, when he married Grandma Betty and never took a drink again. When asked why he stopped his sinful ways, Papa Jim said he was drunk one night, walking home near a graveyard, when he wandered into it and passed out on a tombstone. While he slept, he dreamed of his life, seeing himself walking in a field full of devils and carrying a large toesack filled with his sins. The sack of sins was tied around his neck. He came to a ditch filled with water that he had to cross before the devils caught him. The sack was too heavy to carry as he jumped across the ditch and he knew if he fell in he would drown, because he couldn't swim. So Papa Jim said that he untied the sack of sins and when he woke he was "saved," a Christian the rest of his life.

Was that what I had to do? Did I need to untie my sack of sins in order to be free from the Devil and this thing that caused me to want to kill myself? I was so confused and in such horrifying, excruciating pain, I could make no rational decisions or evaluations of my life.

I chose not to see Gary and the boys and take no phone calls. I was too ashamed to face the wonderful man I loved and the sons I had betrayed, especially Shane, whose hurt was so deep. Monty was thankful his mama was alive and that was all that mattered. But Shane wanted me dead, and he suffered much guilt for that. I had been informed by Ann that Gary and the boys had seen another counselor twice and I would later be given the choice of either hearing their meetings or seeing them on video if I so wanted. "No, I don't want to see them," I assured her.

I drank can after can of Enfamil, all day and night. I smoked packs of cigarettes, ate fruit, drank more Enfamil, suffered more pain.

A few days later, while walking with Ann, I could bear the pain no longer. Even the Demorol only helped so much. I crumpled to the floor. "I can't take another step. I'd rather die." I was sick. Couldn't they see that, for the love of God? I was physically sick and needed medical attention, not psychiatric care. My God! Were these people not human? Had they no compassion?

"I can't move, Ann," I went on. "I'll have to crawl to

my room. Help me, Ann. I can't take it anymore."

She looked down coldly at me on the floor. "Why not, Jean? Too weak? You put the poison in you—now you'll have to learn to take the pain."

"Please! Please, Ann," I begged. "Help me. I'm a human being. You treat me like a dog. All of you do. For God's sake, help me. You'd help an animal. You'd *shoot* an animal to end its misery. Have that much compassion for me. Either kill me or help me."

"Suit yourself, Jean," she called as she walked away. "Lie there in your misery."

I screamed out, "You bitch! You rotten, mean bitch. I don't need you sonofabitches. Fuck you all, you rotten bastards. I'll show you."

She roared with a hearty laugh that filled the halls and brought patients and staff out of their rooms to stare at us. "You'll find that cursing in here doesn't help, Jean. We're used to it."

"You ain't heard nothin' yet, bitch!" I screamed back. "These sick bastards! What do they know? They're too weak to piss. Can't make a decision to save their worthless lives. Dependent on you bastards for even the bath they get. Don't you stare at me, you insane sicko! You people make me wanna puke!"

"Good going, Jean," Ann called. "What a filthy mouth you got. Sounds like a man, doesn't she, you guys? See that little boy haircut?"

"Yeah," somebody yelled. "A boy."

"Fuck off, all of you. It's *my* hair."

"Looks like a lawnmower run over it. You cut it, Jean?"

"None of your fucking business, Ann. I've had it

with you."

Ann walked back to me. I managed to pull myself up against the wall.

"Shut up. I'll get to my room. I don't need you to help me. And I sure as hell don't need them."

"Jean likes rat poison, gang." Ann smiled at them, as the patients had narrowed the distance between us. The staff just stood back, mumbling.

I clung to the wall to keep from falling. I heard every word I was saying, but it didn't sound like me. The voice was strangely hard and bitter and yet, yes, I knew the woman who was saying them.

"You don't know me, Ann, so just shut up."

"We never knew you before on all your trips here, Jean," she said. "But now we're starting to. She's a regular bitch, isn't she?"

"Certified! Bonafide! Bitchyfied! And every other 'fied!' And you don't really wanna know me, Ann. So get the fuck off my case and let me crawl to my room. I'm not proud, baby. I don't mind crawling. But begging I don't do."

I rattled on, hearing snickers from the patients. All it did was give me strength as I inched along the wall, closer and closer to my room. It was farthest from the nurses' station. My anger brought on a horrible shaking of my body. If only I could make it to the door.

"Acts like a man!" a patient called. "Boy haircut!"

"You still on that, you sicko?" I called back, never turning my head. My voice echoed. "She should know, gang," Ann said. "Come on. Get closer, patients, so we can see her fall on her face. Miss Hotshot, queen of the mental hospitals."

I managed to inch to a door and cling to it. "Shut up. You've been on my case since I got here. Now lay the hell off."

They were several feet behind me. I heard the shifting of weight as their feet moved across the tile floor. There must have been eight or ten patients, five or six staff members and Ann was leading the herd. I hated her. I wished she was dead.

As these thoughts came to my mind, I began gasping for breath, trying to stop the panic rising inside me. I couldn't. I was coming apart, turning into someone else. Someone who cursed and fought. Someone like. . . No! I couldn't allow that to happen! They had to see that I was a good little girl. Jeanie Small was a good little girl! Couldn't they see that? Didn't they know I would mind them and never say a word?

My hands came away from the doorway. I was flinging them wildly in every direction, as if fighting the air I could not feel or see. Suddenly I was not longer aware of the pain in my legs, the burning in my chest from the poison. Blindly, I took wild steps around my room, arms flying. I cursed in furious combinations that even I couldn't understand. Words came in choking torrents, screams, cries of anger and frustration!

I slowly became aware of my hands and arms ripping at my red flannel pajamas. The staff had allowed me to wear only heavy sleeping clothes for my walking exercises. I tore pieces of the flannel from my body and flung them about the room. I moved crazily in no particular direction, anywhere and everywhere; I was totally out of control. My pajamas were now ripped to shreds and mostly off my body. I had torn off the legs, ripped them up. My arms felt hot like fire, so I yanked the top off, too. Then I threw my arms around my breasts to hide them. I was crying and cursing so hard I couldn't breathe.

"I—I—I—!" Gulping for air, I tried to speak. "I hate—clothes with holes. Help me! Help me! Mama! Mama! Come get me! They're after me! Please help me, Mama!" Again, I slumped to the floor. Ann came to my side and tried to hold me down.

Patients helped her, as did other staff members. Lifting my body from the floor and onto the bed, they wrapped me in blankets. I was shaking all over and hyper-ventilating.

"It's okay, Jean," Ann assured me. "It's okay, baby."

"Maybe we went too far this time," a pretty, dark-haired staff member said.

"No!" Ann was adamant. "This is what Jean had to do. You know that, Mary Jo. Get the paper bag! Quick! Bring me a Stelazine shot and ten milligrams of Valium. Hurry, Mary Jo."

"Mama! Help me! Come for me! Don't make me do it, Mama! I can't! I can't hurt you! Mama! Mama! I love you, Mama!" I screamed out.

I felt the paper bag being pushed against my mouth and I tried to breathe slowly, in and out, to stop the hyper-ventilation. Ann and the others in the room spoke softly to me, words I couldn't comprehend. My mind was racing.

I saw tiny bits of my life as a child whirling about, and for a fleeting second or two, Mama was there holding me in her arms.

Ann gently pulled my hair back. For a second I saw myself standing in front of the mirror in my bathroom at Gary's and my home. I was staring at the woman with long ponytails tied with rubber bands and ribbons on either side of her head. I looked forlorn, like a child lost. I reached for the scissors, quickly cut off the ponytails and watched them fall into the sink. Then I threw the rubber bands away and played with what was left of my hair. I started to cut more and more, shaping till it looked like of Peter Pan. Suddenly, I realized Gary would hate it. He loved my long hair, as did Monty and Shane. But I couldn't go around looking like a child anymore. I was in my thirties. Looking in the mirror again, though, I noticed I looked even more childish.

The Stelazine shot burned in my arm and I swallowed the Valium Ann put in my mouth. Within minutes, I was calm and, for the first time, ashamed to face her and the other patients.

"Jean's okay now, guys," she told them. "Go ahead and tell her what we always tell a new patient."

I glanced over at them. There were at least five or six still in the doorway. They took a step toward me. "Please speak from there; Jean's so weak." Ann assumed they were going to tell me what a bitch I was and curse me out again.

A giant of a man with a boyish face who was retarded and had spent most of his life being institutionalized, wandered in circles. His head bowed, his huge, black hands making funny shapes, he finally giggled at me and said, "We love you, Jeanie."

It touched my heart that this man-child and the others could find forgiveness within themselves and say those words to me. After all I'd said. I could not speak or return any comment. My eyes filled with tears, but I made no sound. Then all of them smiled at me and, nervously twitching about, repeated his words.

"We do love you, Jeanie. Just like Big John said."

Then they told me what their names were and said they would pray for me, my sons and husband. "We love all patients."

"Don't eat no more rat poison, Jeanie," a blond-haired, blue-eyed girl named Lori said. "We hate to see you in pain. Your legs is right bad, ain't they, Ann?"

"Yes, Lori, they are," Ann said. "Jean's very sick right now. Sick in body as well as mind. First we have to get her body healed, then all of us can help her with her mind. Right, gang?"

"Yeah, Ann!" they chimed in like students. "We will, too."

"Now tell Jean the other things we always tell new patients," Ann counseled.

"Can I do it, Ann? Can I?" Big John asked.

"Yes, John. You're a good spokesman for everyone."

This time Ann didn't stop him when he stepped closer to my bed, where I lay still trembling. He smiled down at me, and I saw the thick lashes surrounding his brown saucer-like eyes, as innocent as a two-year -old's, yet he was as old as I was.

"In here—," he stuttered, "we are—we all the same—he same, Jean. I—in here we—we with—our own people. *Our* people. Right, Ann? Right?"

She patted him lovingly on the shoulder, and walked the patients from the room. I wanted to tell them I was sorry, that I loved them too, that I prayed they would forgive me for cursing them. But no words came. I was choking on tears.

Ann returned a few minutes later. She gave me a shot of Demoral and opened a can of Enfamil, putting a straw in it. She held the can while I, terribly thirsty, drained it instantly. She got another can, gave it to me and I drank it all as well. When she was sure I had calmed down, she pulled a chair up to the bed. She wasn't a woman to make small talk. If it wasn't going to help a patient, she felt no need to waste her breath.

"Is there anyone you want me to contact, Jean?" she asked. "You refuse to see your sons and Gary. You don't want your mother calling here. You refuse to take her calls."

"I wish I could see my Mama." I cried.

Ann looked puzzled. "Your Mama? But you won't take her calls, Jean."

"Not my Mother. My *Mama*," I told her.

"They're not the same person?"

"The same body—but not the same heart or feelings or love. I guess Mama died the night my father died." I turned my head away.

Ann didn't probe any further. She changed the subject.

"Do you have these attacks often?" Ann asked. I turned my head back toward her.

"Sometimes I curse, scream and cry, ripping my clothes off in the end. Gary says it's my 'devil attacks,' that mean woman inside showing the world she ain't gonna take no more pain. I have them more and more now. Out of nowhere they come. I lose all touch with reality. All control. I get so sick of myself, I throw up at times. I just puke and puke."

Ann lifted my hand and held it in her palm as she rose. She was firm, yet warm and comforting. "Dr. Wintermeyer will want to talk with you about this, and you and I will discuss all that later in one-on-one therapy, Jean. You've already been on the ward five days. I don't have much time left to try and help you. Committed patients have their day in court after twenty-one days. And besides, I'll be leaving before you do."

"Leaving?" She was going to leave me, too. "But . . ."

"My husband's in the military, Jean. Naval officer. He's being transferred to California next month."

I flushed angrily. She sighed when I said nothing.

"Oh, hell! Time to move on anyway. I've been here six years. I told them when I took this position as head psychiatric nurse and put my life on the line for you sickos, we did it my way or *else*."

I had to smile. I knew she was teasing. Even then, there was concern and love in her voice for us "sickos." I wanted to tell her I felt betrayed when she said she was leaving, but instead I changed the subject. "You all set me up," I said, beginning to understand. "So that's your way?" I asked.

"Unorthodox, to say the least," she smiled. "But you know what, Jean? You were so nice when you first got here it was sickening. You never moved off course of that damn childlike niceness. Nauseating, I tell you. You had to get the rest of your feelings out, the other personalities within you, or we couldn't help you."

"I don't know how to handle anger, Ann. I lose control. I'm frightened of myself. I don't know who I am. It's like I'm a stranger."

She turned to go. "That stranger is your best friend right now, Jean. No one can hold so much anger inside and heal. I hadn't told you—I didn't feel you were strong enough to hear it—but Gary and the boys refuse to see you, also. They've reached the breaking point too, honey. Rest now."

Okay, Mama, I thought as I was drifting off. You win. I lost you. You left me or died or whatever. Now Gary and my dear sons have left, too. You were right, Mother! Yes *you*, Mother, not Mama. I ended up all alone like you said I would. Are you happy now, Mother?

VOICES OF
STRANGERS

I tossed and turned in a sleep filled with the past's all-too-real nightmares. In one, I was in a car with Gary and the boys.

"Get the snakes off me, Gary." I pleaded.

"What snakes, Jean?"

"There. Can't you see 'em? They're on the floor. They're trying to crawl up my legs. Please, Gary."

"You can't go on like this, Jean."

"They're coming up—they're on my—they're all over me, Gary! Get 'em off. Get 'em off! Hurry, Gary. I can't stand them crawling over me—Gary! Monty! Shane! Help Mama. Please help Mama. Where's my Mama, Gary?"

"You're crazy, Jean!" he shouted. "Don't do this to us. Pay her no attention, boys. She just swallowed too many Elavils. She's hallucinating. Jean, I should have you committed tonight. I should take you back to the asylum. Maybe a trip there would bring you to your senses."

"No, Gary. Don't. I'm begging. Please. I'll be good.

I'll drink coffee, throw up, whatever you say, Gary." I was scratching my body raw, nails digging into my flesh. "Help me get 'em off, though. I *hate* snakes. God! Where's Mama, Gary? I want my mama."

He reached over from the driver's seat and grabbed by arm. "Jean, your mother is at her home in upstate New York. Now please pull yourself together."

"I'm sorry, honey; I'll be a good girl. I swear. You know I'm a good girl when I want to be. Ask Mama. I'm a really good girl. Jeanie is a good girl. Just get the snakes off me." More memories flooded over me as I lay in a drugged sleep.

From the time we are born till the time we die, our lives are filled with images planted forever in our minds. These good and bad images form a kaleidoscope, a menagerie of scenes from childhood.

I should be over my fear of Daddy, but I'm not. His breathing, the sounds his shoes made walking across the porch, his drunken laughter coming from the yard crowded with his whores and buddies, the backdoor slamming as his anger began, the lashes from his belt, the pain, the pain.

And pictures of my dear mama. Mama was my salvation and I thought I was hers, but really we were both victims who used each other's strength to unite and survive. The mistake I made was in thinking that we were united forever, that we were as one and it could never be any other way. Our souls and minds, even our bodies were one, or so the child Jeanie Small believed. Together in fear, together in pain, living like parasites off each other. But I was the worst parasite, draining Mama of all her identity.

Those thoughts faded. Now, I saw a cold night long

ago. The ground lay frozen. I heard small, quick footsteps crossing into the field by our house. For a while, I lay immobile in the bed I shared with Dora and Mattie. Then I found the courage to move from the feather mattress, crawling so as not to wake my sisters, and peep from the ice-streaked window. There was just enough moonlight out to see Mama's frail figure. I was afraid she'd become lost in the dried corn stalks. Fear gripped me. I could not sleep till I knew she was safely back home. So I waited. And I waited.

Then, I heard louder feet moving through the field. Mama and Daddy came into view. He was holding her roughly against his drunken body. They entered the kitchen and he began beating her. They were arguing. She had followed him out into the field where he was in the company of Mama's best friend, a married woman. I heard her pleading with him, and then the sound of her cries as he hit her. Finally, I couldn't bear her pain anymore. I snuck back to the bed and crawled under the quilts, covering my head, burying it and plugging my ears to drown out the anguish of Mama's cries.

Even at that young age, fear had already taken control of my mind and body. It had infected every bone and muscle, strung like a spider's web throughout my nervous system. I was already entering that world of terror where my mind couldn't take reality and I had to escape into another, nearly neurotic personality. It was my shield from pain and suffering. I knew even then that I was different from my sisters, but I never knew how, really.

My mind tumbled to another scene. In it, I became acutely aware of something odd and strange in my behavior. It was on a hot, sultry day in July. Our house was way up in the field off the main road, and it was Mattie's and my chore to check the mailbox daily. We loved it. There was something so exciting about opening the box to see what treasures it might hold.

So, even though the heat was awful, I dragged myself down the ruts in the field and made my way to the mailbox. There were a handful of colorful papers and a catalogue for Mama from Sears and Roebuck as well as a Simplicity dress pattern she'd ordered for twelve cents. Then I saw it. A large, yellow envelope with an incredible message printed on the front in large black letters:

"Congratulations! You have just won Twenty-Five Thousand Dollars. Open im—"

My heart raced. It pounded in my chest. I had no idea what that next word was and I began running up the rut road to the house. I had dropped most of the rest of the mail, but I didn't have time to pick it up. Suddenly, a familiar burning sensation came over me. I started ripping the sundress handed down to me from different cousins. I felt my fingers enter the holes and rip and tear till it was barely hanging from my shoulders. I couldn't stand that, so I yanked it off, leaving me wearing only my white cotton step-ins. "Mama!" I yelled.

She ran in, exclaiming, "Jeanie, what have you done to your clothes? "You have to stop! He'll kill you."

"But, Mama!" I said happily. "You're rich! You can buy me lots of pretty dresses, now. See, Mama. See?"

I handed her the envelope and, after glancing at it, she tore it to bits.

"Jeanie! Lord, honey, this is junk mail. Not worth the paper it's printed on. Do you understand?"

"No, ma'am, Mama."

"They just want me to order things. Oh, Jeanie. What am I going to do with you? I know you have good intentions, but this isn't real. It's just advertising. Now, no more!" she scolded. "No more tearin' off your clothes! I mean it!"

"Yessum, Mama. I'm sorry."

I was. Not only about the envelope which had seemed so wonderful, but about my habit of tearing things up with holes in them. It followed me all my life. I'd go naked before I'd wear any clothing with even the smallest hole in it. To this day, when I open my mailbox and find large yellow envelopes exclaiming I have won millions, I still think it's true.

I was spinning in and out of sleep, now. When I was awake, I was walking the halls with Ann, trying to regain strength in my legs. I lived in the hospital this way for nearly two weeks. I sat in group therapy, not talking, listening to the others. They went on outings, I wasn't allowed to go, for fear I was still suicidal. I had no contact with Gary or my sons, though Ann told me they called often to see how I was. She assured me they loved me, but had finally reached their limit and could not be around me. In a strange way, I felt relieved.

After those two weeks, I had gained a lot of strength and began walking at a slow trot. I couldn't wait till my legs were back in shape so I could jog around the horseshoe-shaped hallway. I told God, "If you'd let me get well, I'll do all in my power to make use of the legs I once took for granted. Still, I was silent a great deal of the time.

Ann came to my room with me one day after our group session.

"You're not taking part in group, Jean," she told me.

"You just sit there, taking up space."

"I have trouble relating to groups of people. I feel it would be better for me to be in therapy one-on-one. I think you feel that way, too. You just don't want to admit it."

"Why wouldn't I?"

"By admitting it, Ann, you'd be saying in essence that I was right about my own mind, that I was well, in tune with what I need and don't need. You'd be admitting that I knew I was extremely sick and felt I knew more about me than you do."

She sighed. "What to do? What to do with Mrs. Brinson? Even if that were true—and I will give you credit, you are very much in tune with some things about your mind—I wouldn't in a million years admit that you knew more than me." She paused and gazed at me. "Now," she said, "I think it's time you heard the tape. I hope you won't miss this chance to really help yourself, Jean."

The tape. What was she talking about? Then I remembered.

"I told you I don't want to see the video, Ann."

She swallowed then said, "The video was destroyed by Gary, Jean. He said they couldn't do that to you. We just have a tape of them talking about their life with you. Not as good as the first video, since they didn't know they were being filmed then. We always perform better if we don't know we're performing, more honestly I think. But it's damn good, Jean. Will you hear it? I'll sit with you."

I gulped down a can of Enfamil and put an unlit cigarette in my mouth. "What if I come apart, Ann? What if I lose it and throw things and break them?"

"Then you'll have to pay for them. They're hospital property, but they can be replaced. But what if you break your mind, Jean? How will you pay for that?"

"By fighting like I've done all my life. Just fighting like hell to survive."

"Then stop beating the hell out of Jean Brinson. Give her some peace. Control yourself. You can do it, Jean."

"Trying to save this one last lost soul before you go, Ann?"

She half smiled. "Will you hear it or not, Jean?"

"Under one condition," I said. "That I can listen to it in the quiet room." A genteel word for the 'padded cell.' "I guess I've heard it all anyway. What could they say I haven't heard?"

"Jean, it's different hearing people talk about you than hearing things during an argument. Remember that. And you know there's no outlet for the plug in the quite room."

"It's the only way, Ann. Run an extension through the crack under the door. I'll feel safe that way."

"I'll see what I can do. Next you'll be asking me if you can have cigarettes in there?"

"Can I?" I asked, trying to return her grin.

"Don't try to manipulate me, Jean. You're good. You're damn good at that. But hell, no, you can't smoke in there. Be back shortly. You do want to hear the tape today?"

"I guess so. There'll never be a 'right' time for it, Ann."

I've heard all padded cells are alike. Having been in several, I'd have to agree. The sole piece of furniture is a mattress on the floor, no sheets or pillows. The walls are bare and grayish. They're cold and without feeling. In this one, there was one small window in the door, perhaps four inches by eight inches with two sheets of thick Plexiglass with wire between them. Your hands would have to be declared lethal weapons to be able to break it. Ann had placed the tape recorder inches from the door so none of the extension cord would be inside the room.

It was black and small like a child's tape player, but it loomed at me like my worst enemy. I pushed the right buttons, turned up the volume and sat on the mattress in the corner up against the cold wall. I heard static, then movement of chairs and people saying things not really meant for recording. Then everything was quiet except for the humming of the machine as it rolled, waiting for the first voice to speak. I wondered who it would be. Gary? Monty? Shane?

"I don't like doing this again." It was Monty's voice coming through the speaker. "It's hard on us, Dad."

"I realize that," Gary said, "but in the end it will be best for all of us, that your Mommy will finally know what we feel."

"We're here to help my wife, Ms. Baker," he told the soft-spoken therapist who I'd never met. "not hurt her. That's the only reason we're doing this."

"And we appreciate that, Mr. Brinson. Just try and say what you feel."

Gary coughed to clear his throat. "I'd like to say we love you, Jean, if you ever listen to this. So don't get mad at us. We just can't go on as a family unless you get well."

"Don't be nice to her, Dad," Shane came in. "Does she care how we hurt or feel? I'm ashamed of her, ashamed to call her Mama."

Gary cautioned Shane, but Miss Baker stopped him. "No. Let Shane and Monty say what they feel, Mr. Brinson, or this is no good." She rustled some papers. "What's your earliest memory of your mother, Shane?"

"Cursing at my Daddy for drinking a few beers," he stated quickly.

"But she loves Daddy," Monty interrupted. "Mom just don't know how to show her love. She gets real mad at little things."

"Does she beat you boys?"

"Just a spanking when we were little," Monty said. "She never really hurt us. She's the best Mama in the world, at times. Sometimes though, she turns into another person. She throws things."

"Mind if I smoke?" Gary said.

"Not at all," Ms. Baker replied.

Gary lit a cigarette and I could hear him get up and start pacing. I could almost feel his frustration.

"We can stay here with you till hell freezes over, Miss Baker, and nothing will change," he said. "In all the times I've brought Jean here, you people who call yourself 'therapists' and 'psychiatrists' have never once helped her."

"Mr. Brinson."

"No. Let me finish. You don't know what she's really like. All the different people inside her. You only see the sad child who tries to kill herself all the time." He exhaled sharply. "Well let me tell you, Miss Baker, what Jean Small Brinson is really like. These idiot doctors walk around with their high-water pants and beards down to their chest and *they* look sicker than my wife."

"Please, Mr. Brinson. We do try."

"Jean Brinson! *My* wife! My sons' Mother! You don't know her. Even I don't know her. The different parts of her fighting within her. Fighting herself, fighting us. She can be a lost child, a gentle, loving woman or a complete bitch.

"Don't get upset, Dad," Shane said. "Remember your blood pressure."

"None of that matters right now, Shane. And don't either one of you answer another question from this woman. I'll do the talking." He was pacing again. "Let's see, now. Where shall I start? Why not while I was dating her, the most beautiful girl I'd ever seen. I loved her from the minute I set eyes on her. But less than two weeks later, I knew there was something wrong with her. I don't claim I knew it was mental illness, but she was strange, different, moody."

"Then why didn't you stop seeing her, Mr. Brinson?"

"I loved her. But there was Sara, her Mother. She and Jean were like one person, with the same mind and thoughts, just different faces. It was sick." He was chain smoking. I could hear him puffing, stamping out one cigarette, lighting another. "But I married Jean in spite of it all. Then she got sicker and sicker and meaner. She hated my drinking a few beers—that's all I ever drink, and I don't hurt a soul—"

"Except Jean, Mr. Brinson?" Miss Baker said.

"I'll forget you said that," Gary told her. "So I'd have a few beers after work with my friends, go home and get the 'third degree' as I called it. First, she'd tear my brain apart by picking at me, having to know every detail. Then, she wouldn't believe me and sometimes she would scratch my face and arms, yelling at *me* to stop. After that, she'd cry and say she was sorry until the next time, which was always just around the corner. Her greatest fear is that she's become a little like R.J. and sometimes, God help me, I think she has."

"Is, or was, that her father?"

"Yes, her Daddy. She's told me and the boys all about him. He was a sonofabitch. Made his family stand against the wall while he pitched a pocket knife at them; beat them all the time. Of course, Jean was a victim, but like all children, what she saw, she learned. I know she's not really like him. I love her Miss Baker, but I don't love all these other people in her head. The Jean I love is a good, decent woman. A devoted wife and mother. But she isn't with us often enough. She goes away for long periods. In her place comes all of the others. Meanwhile, she's getting more and more sick. These days, she can't eat with us. Eats in the kitchen at the counter while we're in the dining room. She can't walk with a glass in her hand—says she gets this burning thing in her brain, gets scared to death and then she throws the glass on the floor or at the wall. I'm afraid for the boys."

"Most mentally ill patients are destructive in some way, Mr. Brinson, but they hardly ever hurt others. Only themselves. It's themselves they hate, not their family."

As if Gary had not heard Ms. Baker speak, he went on.

"Then she runs to the bathroom and locks the door. Stays in there forever. Or runs to our room and hides in the closet or under a blanket in a corner. I go and try to talk to her, but she stares right through me like she don't even know I'm there. For hours, she'll stay in there."

"And we hate her for it!" Shane said. "I wish she was dead. She's hurt us so much. I hate her!"

"*I* don't," Monty said. "'Cause she cries a lot too, don't she, Daddy? When she runs to her room we hear her crying a lot. She don't sound like our Mama then—Dad says she sounds like a child, a little girl. And she does, Miss Baker. So how can I hate my Mama when she's sick and a child like us? I can't; I love Mom."

"And well you should, Monty," Miss Baker told him. "You have that right. And at the same time, your brother Shane has the right to feel he hates her. He doesn't really wish your mother was dead, do you, Shane? You just want that hateful woman to die and leave her in peace so that you can be a family. Right?"

Shane was moving restlessly in his chair. "I don't know. I just hate her, that person she is. I just wish she'd leave us alone."

"But I hope you understand that your mother is a very sick woman. Do you realize that she was abused as a child? That she is in constant pain and that her mind doesn't work like yours or your dad's or Monty's?"

Gary spoke. "How can you expect him to understand, woman? He's just a boy. Even you people don't understand her."

"I don't know Jean, Mr. Brinson," Miss Baker told him. "But I saw her when she was in ICU and in her room, semicomatose. I've read her case history. Even though I don't work with the patients, I work with their families and try to get them to participate in therapy."

Gary laughed a sad laugh, "When will the bitch and all the others go away? When will the Jean we love come back?"

I heard the door slam and the tape went dead. A loud clicking sounded in the room, echoing in my mind. My brain was ablaze with anger, I was hurt! I didn't know these people in that little black box. Who were they? And who was that woman they talked about who was so mean and cruel?

I got up and picked up the recorder, removing the

tape from its carriage. It was still warm in my hand. I sat down on the mattress, still holding it and staring at it. In a surge of hate, I lost control and tore it from its wheel, winding it around and around my hands until they were red and sore.

I made my way to the door, opened it and ran down the hall to my room. Ann saw me and rushed to my side. I took the destroyed tape from around my hands and threw it at her.

"Jean," she said. "Calm down."

"I don't know those people or the woman they were talking about. You gave me the wrong tape. You did it to be mean. I hate you, Ann."

She tried to console me, but I moved away. She said, "No, Jean. We're trying to help you. And you *do* know them. They're not strangers—they're victims Jean, just as you once were."

CHAPTER
15

SEARCHING
FOR THE KEY

Ann was leaving that day. At four o'clock, she would walk out those double iron doors and I'd never see her again. I had really been testing her patience during the time I was in the hospital. I'd lost my temper and thrown my dinner tray many times. The last time was only a few days before this. She had looked at me, shaken her head and walked off. Half an hour later, I was still sitting on the floor trying to pick up the mess. She returned to the dining area and sat at the table.

"Why do you keep throwin' the dinner tray, Jean?" she asked.

"If I knew that, Ann, I guess I wouldn't be doing it," I told her. "You're the psychiatric nurse—you tell me."

"I don't have all the answers, Jean. And we've only made a beginning working together. Now I'm afraid time is running out, but I—"

"My time ran out long ago, Ann. Even Gary and the boys are uncomfortable around me now."

"How would you feel in their place, Jean? You better start getting it together, girl, before you lose your family forever. They love you, Jean. Let them love you."

Suddenly, my mind went back to Ann's question about why I threw the tray.

"I think it's because of the glass, Ann." I said.

"What are you talking about?" Ann asked, not realizing I had changed the subject.

"The dinner tray. I hate glass. It scares me to death. And I hate carrying things in my hands across a room."

"But there has to be a reason, Jean. Like when you're putting together a puzzle, you have to find the right piece. When you're carrying the tray or holding a glass, what are you thinking?"

"I don't know. I'm just scared I'll drop it and somebody'll beat me for it. Maybe it's the past cropping up again. I keep remembering my sister Mattie trying to get the big jar of peanut butter where Mama had stored it—high on top of the tin dish cabinet. Mattie was maybe two; I was four or so. She's climbing on the chair, then she's standing on the bottom shelf, then she tries to crawl higher and the cabinet falls over. All Mama's dishes break all over the kitchen."

"That's good, Jean. Did you just remember that?"

"No. I see it a lot, but I just realized the connection."

"What happens then?" She was now on the floor helping me clean up my mess. Her hand touched mine as she helped me lay the broken glass on my tray. "See, Jean. Just let me help you. Let your family help you. It's a step in the right direction." She sighed. "Now tell me what happens after Mattie turns over the cabinet?"

"I don't really know. She starts crying, screaming—

and I can't stand her crying."

"Why not? Are you afraid you'll be beaten for what she did? Were you in charge of her?"

"I don't know. I start shaking my head wildly; it's bobbing so hard it'll come off my neck soon. My eyes are blinking really fast. The next thing I know, I'm in Mama and Daddy's room hiding behind Mama's sewing machine. I'm covering my eyes with both hands, not wanting to see him when he comes in."

"You mean your Daddy?"

"Yes. I hear him coming up the porch steps—hear the old log cabin door rattle as he opens it—but I can't see his face. Just the sound of his boots and harsh breathing. I can't recall ever leaving my hiding place that day."

She sighed. "Maybe you never did, Jean. You've been hiding all your life."

Together, Ann and I lifted my dinner tray full of food and broken glass and carried it to the trash can.

"Think so, huh?" I said.

She nodded. "You gotta learn to accept yourself for what you are—all the things, not just the good. You have to deal with them no matter how painful." We took two cups, filled them and sat at the table sipping cold coffee.

"It's just so damn hard, Ann. I wonder why I have these feelings. Why not Dora or Mattie?"

"You wouldn't really wish your torment on one of your sisters, would you, Jean?"

"No! Not on anyone."

She walked me down to my room and stood in the doorway for a while. "You have even abused me, Jean. Abused our friendship. You try to manipulate me to get your way. When it doesn't work you sulk the rest of the day."

"I never meant to, Ann. I'm sorry." A picture of Daddy flashed through my mind. "He beat me and Dora with hoes, you know?"

"Hoses?" she asked.

"Hoe handles. The handles of hoes. When we didn't chop the cotton right, or weed the tobacco right, or hoe the garden right, he'd beat us across the stomach with the hoe handle. Mama was always scared it would make our periods not come. Dora was menstruating then. I wasn't. Mama was scared we wouldn't be able to have babies one day."

Ann came back to the bed where I was sitting. "You see, Jean, you have so much insight into your mental illness. You're the kind of patient psychiatrists love; you enable them to help you because you have all the answers locked inside just waiting to be found."

"God! The things I have locked within me are enough to kill someone. One good thing about Mother's heart attack and stroke is they've impaired her memory."

"Would you like me to call her, Jean?" Ann asked. "Do you think you could talk to her now?"

"To Mama yes, to Mother no! I don't expect you to understand that, Ann. But it makes perfect sense to me and right now 'me' is all I got."

"You're wrong. You have Gary and Shane and Monty and a lot of friends—"

"Maybe family, Ann, but no friends. People like me, crazy women, don't have friends. No one ever knows how to take you or what you'll do next. I've lost it too many times and I've lost all my friends."

She looked at her watch. "Time for me to go, dear. But I want you to promise me you'll keep searching for the right key, the one that will unlock the door to Jean Brinson's mind and her personal hell. Find that key, sweetheart, and you'll find help. If you don't, you'll live the rest of your life in misery. And lay off the damn rat poison; there really aren't any good nutrients in it."

We laughed together for the first time since I got there. "I promise," I said seriously. "I'll keep searching for the key to the maze."

The time had come for her to walk down to my room and say goodbye. I waited for her to come until I had become a nervous wreck, long past four o'clock. I brushed my hair, tried to put on a bit of makeup, then decided to go find her. At the nurses' station, I asked about Ann and someone handed me a note sealed with a piece of tape. Hurriedly, I took it back to my room, wondering what was inside. I sat in the chair by the bed, turned on the lamp, removed the tape and began to read.

Jean,

I'm sorry. I hate goodbyes. I pray you will get better and find the key we talked about. Please don't get upset, but since I'm the head psychiatric nurse, I have been told by the judge you'll be seeing upon your release that he will order you to seek psychiatric help outside the hospital. If you fail to do so, a warrant for your arrest will be issued. You'll be picked up, and Jean, he won't send you back here, but to Columbia. Bull Street, "The Big Rock," as it's called. So I'm giving you this phone number of a doctor I know. She's a wonderful therapist. If anyone can help you, she can. For your sake if not for Gary and the children, please call her. I will always remember you, Jean. Not for what you are, but for that little lost girl in you wanting to get out.

Love, Ann

I folded the note and put it in my purse. So it would be mandatory that I see a therapist. I'd have no choice! Wasn't that the story of my life? Doing what others told me? Everybody thought I was crazy. Now a judge I'd been in front of a few times would demand I see a therapist once weekly or more. And if the therapist felt I needed it, I could be committed again.

I'd be hauled off to the state asylum like a caged animal.

Okay, I told myself. I'll do what they want. I'll be a good girl from now on. I'll attend all the group sessions; I'll have one-on-one therapy with the head psychiatrist; I'll eat all my meals and not throw my tray even if I have to put it on the floor and drag it; I'll attend all doctors' and patients' meetings in the day room and I'll converse with the others. Whatever they wanted me to do, I'd wind myself up like a doll and do it. Anything to "pass the judge," as we patients called it.

In late November, two days after Thanksgiving, I had my hearing in court. There were two large desks below the judge's platform. One desk was for Gary and the boys, the other for my court appointed attorney and me. Two psychiatrists sat at another, smaller table. They testified, after having spent a few minutes with me in another room. Both of them agreed I desperately needed counseling, but not by just a therapist from County Hospital or someone still in training. It had to be a board certified psychiatrist or psychoanalyst, either in private practice or a staff doctor at a private hospital. My attorney asked if I understood. I whispered, "I do."

The judge asked some questions about me. My attorney was my only spokesperson. Patients were never allowed to speak in court.

Judge Fields began to speak, looking directly me, then glancing at Gary, Shane and Monty.

"After hearing testimony from both Dr. James Ward and Dr. Samuel Green, it is my opinion that the patient, Jean Small Brinson, seek private psychiatric help within a period of no longer than five days from November 26, and that her professional help will continue until such time this court and a panel of doctors, including the one she will choose, has decided either in her absence or with her present that she is no longer a threat to herself."

My attorney said, "Agreed, your honor."

"Agreed, John?" Judge Fields asked, puzzled. "Well, this certainly sets a precedent. You arrogant attorneys usually argue with the court and its appointed doctors. I'll remember this, John, whenever you try to get an amendment passed in my domestic courtroom. I thought you were for the patient."

John half rose and nodded at Judge Fields. "I am, Your Honor. Just like the court is."

Judge Fields looked me straight in the eyes, "Mrs. Brinson, I'd like to say a few things to you before this court is recessed. You have been here three or more times. That hurts. But what really disturbs me is this wonderful family you have here standing by you, giving their support. I won't scold you or attempt to make you look ignorant, not intentionally. You must use all your strength to get well and be a responsible person. But I say to you this day that if you ever appear in my court again because of being committed, I will personally send you to Columbia for no less than a year. I hope and pray to our Blessed Savior you know what you have done by your behavior to these fine boys and Mr. Brinson." All I could do was nod my head. "Good. Because doctors or attorneys won't help you if you are in my court again. I trust you understand, Mrs. Brinson."

Again John half stood. "Yes, Your Honor. She does."

"Then it is so ordered this day that Mrs. Jean Small Brinson seek professional help and have her therapist keep in touch with this court." He looked out at Gary and the boys. Shane was stiff as a board, but Monty was weeping softly. "Mr. Brinson, I will remember you, these boys and your wife in my prayers. God be with the three of you. If your wife becomes suicidal again, call me as soon as possible. She will be arrested immediately." He rapped his gavel. "This court is adjourned."

We all rose to leave and I walked over to my sons. I tried to hug Shane, but he walked away. There was so much pain and confusion in his young eyes. I hugged Monty, who was still weeping.

On the ride home we were very quiet; when we did talk, it was strained and uncomfortable. I sensed a dreadful uneasiness about Gary. He seemed weary and tired from all the years of hell I'd put him through. I reached over, took his hand and let it rest in my palm. It gave me reassurance and counteracted some of the shame I felt. Gary was such a wonderful man, but living with my demons had nearly destroyed the gentle and kind person I fell in love with. When we arrived, he carried my luggage into the house while the boys went about their chores, feeding the dog and taking out trash. While we were unpacking Gary reached over and kissed my face. He looked so sad, so tired. Just worn out.

I tried to prepare dinner, but my legs were still too

weak to stand for long. Gary and the boys pitched in to help. We cooked together, set the table together and ate together for the first time in so long. It was a simple meal of burgers and fries, but to me—finally back home—it was a dinner fit for kings. Even with all the emotional troubles going on between us, that was one of the happiest meals we ever shared. Maybe all we had left was the love and honesty between us.

"What's that mess you're drinkin', Mom?" Shane asked. "Is it eggnog? Looks nasty."

I explained, "It's calcium to replenish my bones." I hoped he'd let it drop. He didn't. He started talking about the rat poison, but Gary hushed him. I winced at the bitterness in Shane's eyes. Monty reached over and slapped his arm.

Shane looked up. "Don't—"

"He's mean, Daddy," Monty broke in. "He wishes Mom was dead, and I hate him and wish he was dead. I hate you, Shane."

"Stop it!" Gary shouted. "Not another word!"

"It's all right, honey," I told Gary. "This isn't fair to any of you. But right now I have no place to go. You children and Gary are all I have. I don't have a job, so I can't afford to move out. Just bear with me till I get stronger and more mentally fit, then I'll leave. I promise!"

Gary threw down his burger. "You'll do no such thing, Jean. You couldn't survive on your own. Me and the boys, we're your life, and by God we'll all stick together till you get the help you need."

Monty smiled in Shane's direction as if he'd won a battle he'd been fighting, perhaps ever since I'd been hospitalized. I assured Gary and my sons I would be calling the therapist, whose phone number Ann had given me, early the next morning. "I promise I'll work hard with her to help myself become the mother and wife you all deserve."

When I called, I was extremely lucky and got an appointment for the next day. Because of my weak legs, I still couldn't drive, so Gary dropped me off and said he'd be back in an hour. The therapist's name was Dr. Carol Wintermeyer, a fine-looking woman in her early forties with auburn hair. She spoke with a slight English accent. She seemed a graceful, elegant lady, and I liked her immediately. She would be my own miracle, all wrapped up in one hundred pounds of warmth and compassion. I called her "Dr. Win," although she was a Ph.D., not a medical doctor.

Dr. Wintermeyer couldn't prescribe my medications, so I had to see my medical doctor on a regular basis for bloodwork. In our first session she assessed my mental state. I wondered what she really thought of me. After that, she scheduled twice-weekly sessions for us. During the following weeks, my life was once again in the hands of a stranger, yet I never felt ill at ease with her. It was as if I had known her all my life. I felt safe, warm and loved around her. Where had this angel of mercy been when my hell on earth was destroying my family and me?

I was fooling myself if I thought it was going to be easy to find the answers, however. I didn't know I would go through an even greater struggle before we finally found that "key" Ann told me about. Later, I would wonder which was worse—my battle with insanity and suicide, or facing the truth.

CHAPTER
16

A PLACE, A ROOM

I was sitting on Dr. Win's reclining chair. She was speaking in a warm, soothing tone. She came over to my chair and reclined it. "Now, I want you to lie back and relax, dear. We'd have done this earlier, but I felt you needed a few sessions before taking this step."

"What step?" I asked.

"I want to take you a place you haven't seen in years—or maybe you have and can't remember it. It's not a painful place, Jean. It will be warm and you'll feel the warmth inside you, hugging you like your Mama. I am taking you to a safe place and you have to believe in me or I can't help you. Do you understand?"

"Yes," I said softly. I stared at a black spot on the ceiling where she pointed. I felt sleepy, yet I knew I had the energy to accomplish whatever it was Dr. Win wanted of me. I lay back in the chair, and felt myself close to the chair's fabric. I knew I wasn't totally hypnotized, for I could still hear the humming sounds of Dr. Win's wall clock and papers being shuffled in her hands, but I paid no attention to them. They held no meaning. The only meaningful things I felt were the safety of that huge, reclined chair and her voice.

"You're going on a little journey, Jean," she said softly. "Along the way you will see many things. People. Places. But whatever you see will not harm you. They are things in your past—things that are dead and can no longer harm you. Even if what you see is painful it can't hurt you now. Above all, you must trust me and know I will allow no harm to come to you. Do you trust me, Jean?"

"Yes, Dr. Win."

"Now take a few very deep breaths."

I was falling deeper and deeper into the fabric of the chair, until it felt like it was my clothing. When she knew I was completely relaxed, Dr. Win said, "Let us go down these long steps, stopping briefly on each one to look around and see if anything is familiar." When I responded "no," we walked further and further down the carpeted steps until I came to a small room.

Together we went in. We filled the room with furniture, old stuffed chairs and chintz sofas like the ones I was used to as a child. Dr. Win placed imaginary colorful plants and flowers around the room, opened all the window shades to let the warm sun flow in. Then she said, "Search the room Jean to see if anyone is there with you." I wasn't surprised to find there was.

"Yes," I whispered. "There's a pretty girl here—long blond hair and the smoothest white skin."

"Do you recognize her, Jean?"

"Yes. She's Jean Brinson. She's dancing, loves the music. It's playing real loud. She's smiling—she's always smiling. So nice. A real nice young lady.

"So is this girl you, Jean? Or maybe just a part of you?"

"She's a piece of the puzzle—you know? She's a good piece, not an ugly ragged one."

"Can you see anyone else, Jean?" she asked.

"Yes. There's this dirty little girl, huddled in a corner. She's afraid, head bowed and hands covering her eyes as if to block out the sun's rays. No! Not the sun! It's the horror of seeing what is in the room. The dirty child is crying very loudly. Then her hands come away from her eyes and she is picking the rickrack from her dress."

"Why, dear?" Dr. Win said.

"It has holes in it. She can't stand clothes with holes. But he'll whip her if he—"

"No he won't, dear. He's not going to hurt her. Do you know this child, Jean?"

"Yes. She looks like me when I was a little girl."

"And is she part of the puzzle?" I nodded. "Is she a good part of it like Jean Brinson?"

"Yes. She's a good girl—just ask Mama. She does anything Mama tells her to. She loves her Mama. She'd die for her. But she's real sad—like she knows something and she doesn't want to know it. I don't know what makes her so sad."

"And do you known her name?"

"Oh yes. She's Jeanie Small. I don't like her sad face. Can I come up the stairs now? I feel afraid and sorry for her. Can I? I'll be a good girl, Dr. Win. Jeanie's always a good girl."

"Can you stay in the room long enough to tell me what becomes of the child, Jean?"

I found myself tensing up. "She gets married and has two boys—Monty and Shane—but she can't be a mother to them."

"Why not, Jean?"

"She's still a child—she never grows up. A child can't be a mother to children. She'll always be a child."

"Does she want to?"

"Sometimes. It's easier if she is a child—then she ain't got grown-up worries. She don't have to explain things to her husband if she's a child."

"What does she look like—when she grows up, I mean?"

"Bigger, but still a child," I said. "Her mother's got a picture of her all grown up—she's wearing a red plaid flannel shirt and white baggy jeans. And she's walking up the stairs, looking back down—with a man's Sunday felt hat on her short hair, pulled down low over her brow, like she's hiding something and she can't tell anybody what it is. Her mother hates that picture—says it's the saddest one she has of Jeanie. So Jeanie asked her mother to tear it up or hide it. But her mother still has it."

"Does Jeanie love her mother?"

"She don't know any mother. She worships Mama, though. And sometimes her and her mama have long talks."

"About good things, Jean?" Dr. Win said. "Or bad?"

"Both. She talks to Jeanie like she's a child. She hugs her and pets her and calls her pretty and writes letters to her that say, 'My dear, beautiful daughter.'"

"So Jeanie is never afraid or uncomfortable around her 'Mama'. Is that right, Jean?"

"Oh no, Dr. Win. Jeanie loves Mama."

"And Mama loves her?"

Something about her question made me nervous. I began trembling. "Oh yes. Jeanie's a good girl—so her mama loves her."

"Relax, Jean, breathe deeply. Just stop thinking about the child Jeanie, look around the room and tell me if anyone else is there with you."

I did as she asked but I couldn't see anyone. Then I heard the cursing, the loud, vulgar mouth of a mean woman. It frightened me at first. I turned my head and saw her. "I see someone now but she looks mean and hateful. She's chain-smoking. She acts like she hates the people in the room, calling all of them bad names. Her face is twisted in hate. I hate looking at her."

"Do you know her?"

"I know her," I said.

In the trance-like state of mind I was in, things became clearer and had a deeper meaning. It was like these things were actually taking place. They were so real. Still I wasn't afraid.

"And do you know her name, Jean?" Dr. Win asked.

"She's Gary's wife," I heard myself say. "She's Mrs. Brinson. She hates it when people call her Jean or Jeanie. She hates everything, mostly herself. She's sick! Mean! She tries to kill herself—and gets committed to asylums. She's all twisted up."

"Does she hurt her family, Jean? Her children? Gary?"

"She curses in front of her children sometimes—but just spanks them—never beats them. When her husband drinks, though, she screams and scratches at him because he won't stop. Sometimes her children and husband hate her. They wish she was dead. I wish she was dead, too. I hate her more than they do. I hate having to live with that hateful bitch. I wish I could throw her in the fire and she'd have to beg for mercy the rest of her life."

"Is that who you're trying to kill when you take poisons and cut your wrists, dear?" Dr. Win asked gently.

"Oh no! She's Mrs. Brinson the mean one—she tries to kill Jeanie the child. She hates that child. She doesn't want to know the things Jeanie knows—secrets, you see. Jeanie has secrets, but she'll never tell them. She promised she won't."

"Who did she promise, Jean?"

"Her mama! Mama is all Jeanie has. She makes promises to her mama. Sometimes Jeanie feels like she's still inside Mama's womb. She's warm in there, loved and protected. She is a part of Mama's body—like they're one person."

"And are they one person—because they share so much?"

"Not like it sounds—they don't share the same body. But Jeanie will always think of them as one person—united forever. Does that make sense?"

"United how, Jean? Their minds? Souls? What?"

"What they share are secrets—secrets they can't ever tell anybody. I mustn't talk about those secrets, but I'll tell another one."

"This lady she calls 'Mother' isn't her 'Mama.' In a way Jeanie's mama died years ago. She still has the same body—her mother—but she's not the same. Jeanie doesn't like this woman she calls 'Mother.' Jeanie's scared to death of her, but she don't know why."

"No? And what do you think, Jean? Why would Jean

152

be afraid of her Mother?"

I felt tears run down my face. I wasn't afraid, though, because I heard the great warmth in Dr. Win's voice. Still, there were things I couldn't say. I knew why Jeanie was scared of her Mother. I knew why she didn't like her, but I couldn't tell Dr. Win. I wouldn't tell anybody. Shaking my head, I quickly changed the subject.

"Mama" was a good, decent farm woman who loved her children, especially Jeanie. She was gentle and kind. But this woman called 'Mother' wore lots of make-up, bright red lipstick and inch-long nails always painted so red. She was picture perfect. Her clothes were perfect. Her eyebrows were penciled in perfectly. Her voice and speech were perfect.

She adored her children, lived her life for them—all except Jean. I knew she didn't like me anymore. We both tried, but our relationship was strained and we were uncomfortable with each other. So even with all her perfections, I hated being around her.

And the fear I felt was awful. I was scared to be in her company. I was petrified I'd say the wrong thing and she'd be hurt or angry and never visit me and her grandsons again.

"I never can say the right words to her," I said. "I stumble all over myself. Gary hates it when I'm childish around her. He says I should act my age and say how I feel. But I can't. 'Mother' is this hard-looking woman with her hair dyed jet-black. However, I realize she's a good woman. I guess I just thought I'd have Mama all my life. I never dreamed she'd die when Daddy did, Dr. Win. I miss her so much, my dear Mama."

Dr. Win stepped close to my chair, never touching it.

"Jean, I'm going to let you leave the room now. Look around and see how pleasant it is so you won't be afraid to enter it again. Feel the sun—its warmth—and know you're safe. It's your room, and it's here just for you. Feel the peace within yourself. Look around and see the things you like and walk to the steps. I'm at the top of the stairs. Now come up to me slowly, as if each step is something that holds beauty and it's hard to let go. You are coming toward the top now, Jean. Lie there and relax. When you feel good about these new surroundings, open your eyes and look at me."

It seemed forever before I reached the top and opened my eyes to see Dr. Win standing over me, smiling. I was tired, but not in a weary way. It seemed as if I had been on a journey that I liked, and now I just wanted to get home and sleep.

"How do you feel, Jean?" she asked, taking my hand. "If you're tired, that's normal. Most patients are."

"Yes I was, but now I'm fine. I wasn't hypnotized, Dr. Win. You can't make me believe I was."

She almost laughed out loud. "That's very perceptive of you, dear. I don't hypnotize, Jean. I do hypnotic suggestions—put patients in a trance-like state of mind."

"It's not the same?" I asked.

"No. A therapist is only as good as her patient will allow her to be. I can only take you places where you already want to go but are afraid to, or don't know how. I can help only if you accept my help. I do not put people in the room, I take you there. Only you can fill the room with those you want or need to see. It's your mind at work—I'm just the instrument that propels you to believe in yourself and not be afraid."

For the first time, I was not afraid of my therapist or anyplace she might take me. My mind was confused though—was I accepting her help because it was court ordered? Or because Gary had given me no other choice? Was I trying to save my marriage, our family and myself from insanity, or just following court orders to keep from being sent to Bull Street?

When I told Dr. Win how confused I was, she assured me that I could not fool her. If I were playing games to keep from going to Columbia, she would quickly recognize it and even more quickly dismiss me as her patient and write a letter to the judge. I had finally met someone who felt great compassion for the abused child I had been and the mentally ill woman I was now, while still having the ability, intelligence and sensitivity to treat the real Jean Small Brinson and to treat her as the adult she wanted to be.

I realized that day that Gary, Monty, Shane, Mother, family members, friends all wanted to help, but they had felt so sorry for me that they had treated me as one would an invalid child. Though I professed the desire to get well, it was easier to accept their pity than to undertake the hardships and feel the pain I would have to relinquish my invalid role. I was neither ready to be responsible for the pain I inflicted, nor as to find a cure for the pain I still felt.

Deep inside, I hated myself. The more I hated myself, the sicker I got. I was living within a vicious circle. Around and around I danced—never making any progress. I was never able to move beyond the circle. Trapped inside it and frantic like Daddy, I was guilty of hurting those I loved most and should have protected. That was the most horrifying and painful thing I would ever have to admit to myself. Even Dr. Win couldn't ease that pain. It was something only I could work through in the future in order to feel better about myself.

In a way, Daddy did not die on that night long ago. He lived on for countless years in my body and mind. He lived on in the others: in little, brutalized Jeanie Small; in the hysterical Mrs. Brinson, defiantly acting out her pain; and in Jean Brinson, the frightened woman who didn't want to live.

When I explained all these feelings to Dr. Win, she said something wonderful to me.

"Now you have a 'room' of your own, Jean. You don't have to be in my office to enter that room. It's there for you anytime you want or need it. Just close your eyes and go there. Discover the real Jeanie Small, as well as the real Jean Brinson. Get in touch with all the parts of your personalities. And remember, dear, no one can enter this place without you allowing them. It's your room."

Dr Win poured two glasses of water and handed me one. I started to take it but withdrew my hand. "I'm sorry, dear. Is the glass dirty?" She asked.

"No, I just can't hold glasses or dishes in my hands. Do you have a plastic cup?"

As Dr. Win was getting one she asked, "Why do you hate glass?"

"I don't really know the whole answer." I told her about hiding behind Mama's sewing machine after Mattie accidentally turned over the cabinet, and about Daddy breaking glasses at my feet.

"I know it has something to do with him and my childhood. But something is missing—a piece of the puzzle."

"Well, as we work, many things will come to you, Jean. Right out of nowhere you'll see and remember things you haven't thought of in years. Many of those things—in fact most of them, will be painful for you, but you must unearth them to help yourself."

"I know," I sighed. "I'm just so tired of people picking my brain. Tired of telling strangers about my life. I don't feel like I have anything that belongs to me anymore."

Still, in other ways I felt better. For the first time, I had a place to call my own. It was a wonderful feeling of freedom. At home I'd find myself trying to take a nap each day, and I usually ended up in the "room." Some days it was so pleasant I never wanted to leave. Others, it was so painful I never wanted to enter it again.

It was one of those times when I was lying in my own bed at home, having gone willingly into the "room," that I suddenly knew the whole truth about why I hated glass. All the horror of its true origin became so clear to me that wondered why I hadn't seen it before. When Mattie turned over the tin cabinet, breaking all of the dishes and glasses and I hid behind the sewing machine, it wasn't me or Mattie Daddy beat.

I could see him clearly now, holding Mama on the floor on top of the broken pieces of glass and china, beating her with his leather belt till there were bruises all over her body. She was punished for *our* childish mistake. That was why I hated glasses and dishes and was petrified to carry them across the room. If I broke them he would beat my precious mama again.

At least one pile of maggots had been removed from the mind, heart and soul of Jean Brinson. But there was still more that would have to come out if I was ever to heal.

17

DADDY

At our next session, as if in preparation, Dr. Win began to ask me about Daddy. "What was it like the last few months before your father died?" Dr. Win asked in her quiet, soothing voice.

"All my life I've put scents to things and people. The only way I can explain it is that there was a strong odor to the last few months of Daddy's life."

Later in my therapy with Dr. Win, I realized that I associate certain smells with the emotion of fear. Sometimes it would smell of the heat of July or the cold death of winter; never did it have the fresh scent of the less extreme seasons.

"Often it had the rank odor of hog slops, since I have many memories of feeding the animals just before he died. Mattie and I would haul the big bucket of slops down the beaten path to the pen. When we arrived at the side of the pen, Mattie would almost cry at the thought of us having to ease our way under the electric fence. I don't think we ever fed the hogs without getting shocked on some part of our bodies.

"More than once, we'd drop the slops and have to cup it with our bare hands to get it into the pigs' trough. It'd slosh about in the trough as we each held one side of the pail. Barefoot, we always managed to get the slops on our feet. I would have to use one foot to cover the other with dirt in order to absorb the stench and mess that made us gag. Still we would press on, knowing they didn't yet have enough food. We'd have to pick weeds or break ears of corn or even pull up hills of Mama's pole beans in one of her gardens. Always we feared Daddy would somehow know if the hogs didn't have enough to eat.

"Daddy seemed to be drinking more and more toward the end of his life. One day in early June, we saw him on the road. I was glad it was summer, as Daddy stayed out later then. Mama would have the protection of darkness. That was our only hope, that he would always come home after dark, because for some time now Mama had sworn she would not just stand there anymore and take his beatings. We'd run to a neighbor's house and take refuge till the late hours, and nearly crawl back into the house when he was finally sleeping. Often we had to wake Mattie because Daddy would bolt the back door so we couldn't enter."

"It must have been so frightening for you," Dr. Win mused.

I nodded. "Hiding behind the outhouse, I watched Daddy stagger up the road. As he came closer to the house, I could smell the whiskey when he whistled. He always whistled, sang and yodeled real loud like he was happy. He was wearing a Sunday pink shirt and gray dress slacks, and on his head was his usual Sunday go-to-meeting gray felt hat. He wore it cocked to the right side of his head. Had he not been drunk and mean, any woman would easily have fallen in love with his handsome, sun-tanned face. He had high cheekbones that twitched as he laughed—or tried to lie to Mama.

"I made my way from the outhouse to the side of the shack and I could see part of his body as he came into the yard. I saw one arm swinging by his side as he staggered, whistling even louder. Even as he approached the rotten porch, his feet stepping on the squeaking boards, he was already calling Mama. It was Mama's practice to wait by a window till she saw him walking up the road or a familiar car bringing him home. This way she could have his supper warmed when he entered the house, thus avoiding a few extra licks with his fist or the belt. I could smell the food coming from the kitchen where she was warming it for his supper. We had eaten long before.

"Mama called out softly, 'I'm in the kitchen, R.J., warming your supper. Come on in here, honey.'

"The screen door slammed as he went to the kitchen. My three brothers, Mattie and Beth were on the floor in the parlor, coloring in some old books given to us. At least that was where I had left them when I'd heard his whistle. Dora had already run away by then. Mama had nobody left to help her but me.

"I listened to the sounds of his feet as he stomped across the sagging floors. Always I could hear him cursing. I had made my way around back of the shack now, my ear pressed against the house to hear when he hit Mama. At times like this, I would bang on the side of the house or throw cans or anything to get his attention so Mama could make a run for it. Her frail, petite body was worn out. She just couldn't take the beatings anymore. But often, he wouldn't hear my commotion, or by the time he did, he'd have already beaten her senseless.

"This particular time, she was putting his supper on his plate. She reached out to hand it to him and I heard the plate slam against the wall. Then all hell broke loose. He began throwing all her dishes and cursing so loud it could be heard far down the road. Mama was crying. The children had run to the kitchen, screaming. I moved closer to the back screen door and looked inside. Mama had warned me that when he was acting this way I was not to enter the house, but to try to run for help. I'd done that several times, but no man in Horry County dared interfere with another man doing what was thought to be his 'manly' duties.

"I tried throwing pebbles, making animal sounds but nothing worked. I screamed through the door to Daddy, 'One of your drinking friends is coming in the yard.' He had Mama on the floor now, choking her and I knew I had to go inside. Screaming, crying, I begged him to stop. Mama just lay there gagging. I began to claw at his back. He flung me off with one hand, still holding her down with the other.

"I heard little Will scream, 'When I get big I'm gonna kill you. Quit hittin' Mama, you sumumabitch!'

"The chairs in the kitchen were turned over and as I tried to scratch at his back again, Daddy fell over in a drunken stupor. Quickly, Mama and I fled into the cornfield. It was the longest journey of my life.

"Though the corn was green and tall and hid our bodies, we knew we weren't safe. This time Daddy was doing something he'd not done before—he was following us after he'd revived. I heard the door slamming, him cursing Mama and me, his Sunday shoes kind of gliding through the rows of corn. Mama and I eased to the edge of the field and squatted so we could see through the plants. He was moving fast for a drunken man. I saw his feet weave in and out of the rows, calling Mama.

"In the distance, I heard the children in the yard crying and begging him to stop. I heard the hogs rooting and grunting in their pen nearby, heard old trucks ambling down the rutted roads, hillbilly music coming from the cars and drunk old men laughing and acting like children. Mama was holding me close to her, begging me to breathe, but I was not with Mama anymore. I don't really know where I was, but I felt as if I were standing back, watching this horror through a black-rimmed window. Yet when I tried to close it out by shutting my eyes, it would not disappear.

"His voice grew louder and closer now. Silently, Mama dragged me with her across the rows of corn. Soon we were coming to the clearing. There was a narrow dirt road and a house sitting about a block off the main road. Mama jerked my arm and we started toward the house. We were halfway there when we realized no one was at home.

"'Jeanie! Jeanie!' Mama cried, pulling me toward the wide ditch filled with slimy green water. 'Hurry! He's seen us! Run, Jeanie! He'll kill me!'

"He was laughing and telling us he had us now. Mama grabbed my arm and pulled me toward the ditch. Together we tried to jump across. Being a long-legged, thin child, I reached the other side, but Mama let go of my hand and was standing immobile in the filthy water. I pulled and tugged at her and finally she climbed up. Now at least we were on the opposite side from him.

"Mama and I had now changed roles without either of us realizing it. It was me who was dragging her up the other side of the ditch and running toward another house in the distance. It was Jeanie the child protecting Mama the child. We ran faster and faster, till we were in our neighbor's yard. They were on their porch, just passing a nice Saturday with iced tea and tobacco. I began begging them to help us—and as quickly as it had begun the nightmare was over. Oh I could hear him on the porch telling the neighbors he was after his wife and girl, that he'd seen us go in their house, and he'd find us if he had to burn down the place. But it wasn't real. He was someone I didn't know hunting two people I didn't know.

"Mama and I had followed Miss Flora Belle Todd into her parlor and then to her bedroom. We were behind the quilts that she had stacked in a corner waiting for their winter cleaning. We were now playing a game. Jeanie Small was there only in her skinny body. Her mind had shifted to another place where she could find safety—hiding in her Mama's closet, not a neighbor's house, her face buried in the clothes and she was now smelling everything in sight and counting in a whisper.

"Smell! Smell! Smell! Sniff and sniff and sniff! Letting the scent of the cloth settle deep into her nostrils. Then the counting. Sniff three times. One! Two! Three! No, that wasn't right. Sniff five times, tapping my nose with the cloth each time. One tap! Two taps! Three Taps! Four Taps! Five Taps! One, two, three, four, five—one, two, three, no! One, two, three, four, five! Now she was satisfied. They smelled of kerosene like her Mama's biscuits.

The smelling and counting went together like hand and glove.

"Then Daddy strode into the room. Miss Flora Belle spoke with him in a low but friendly and gentle manner, assuring Daddy that his wife and girl Jeanie were not there. I heard him shout at her, 'You're lying! I saw them run inside.' But he was just guessing. She'd made us go through the back door. She just smiled at him, because farmers 'don't mess in another man's affairs, especially when it's between him and his wife.' The unspoken part of her sentence still stung the back of my mind— 'because a man's wife is his property, like the shirt on his back, and he can and is even expected to beat his family and keep them in line.'

"I don't know when he left, but finally I moved from behind the stack of quilts and sat in a straight-backed wood chair, waiting for Miss Flora's husband, Carl, to take us to Mama's sister's house. As we waited for Carl to dress and get his wallet, I started counting and sniffing again. Miss Flora came over to us.

"'What's wrong with your girl, Sara? Is she sick?'

"'No ma'am, Miss Flora,' Mama said. 'She has a lot of awful habits. He'd kill her if he saw her doing that— stop it, Jeanie! Thank you, Miss Flora, for hiding us. I reckon one day he'll kill us, or me. Stop that smellin', Jeanie!' Mama scolded and slapped my hand. 'She'll quit in a minute; she's right nervous still.'

"Mr. Carl drove us to Aunt Emma's and Daddy came for us the next morning. We had no automobile at that time, so a neighbor had loaned him his pickup to fetch us home. Mama fixed breakfast for all the children, and Daddy made us search for every egg we could find in the henhouse and woods. After eating, he got dressed and started walking toward town. Mama just looked at me sorrowfully when he went out. We both knew what lay ahead when he returned.

"Once again, I got that feeling that I would get often in my life. It seemed like my face was pinkish, with a glow of warmth covering me. I had the overpoweringly soothing sensation that I was still inside Mama's womb. It was so protective and warm, I never wanted to leave and I could almost feel the water in her stomach. It was as if I'd never been born and was still a clean and good thing and nothing dirty had ever touched me.

"Mama's silky long black hair flowed about her shoulders; her milky white skin was smooth as satin, and as we cleaned the kitchen, me right behind her every step, I felt we were the same person. In my mind, I kept telling her of my great love for her and that I would gladly kill Daddy for her or die for her.

"'I love you, Mama! I love you.' I repeated this out loud, over and over, but wrapped in her other thoughts, Mama never responded.

"He came home just before sundown, while the lightbugs were still tapping against the screens and gnats swarmed on the porch. He was drunk, but not in a stupor. He ordered all the boys to bed, crying. Then he made Mama and us girls form a line in the parlor. He whipped out his leather belt and began hitting us as we marched in a circle until he stopped. Bruises all over us, we crept to bed.

"The next day, I was helping Mama hang out the wash. She was mostly silent, staring at Daddy off plowing in the field. He had his khakis rolled up to the knees and his straw hat was pulled low on his brow to keep away the blistering sun. Once in a while, he'd yell at the mules and strike them with a leather whip, just as he'd beaten us the night before. Then he'd start to whistle, as if he'd had a pleasant weekend and just started off a fine week of work. I was lost in the moment and didn't really hear Mama when she began speaking.

"'What, Mama?' I asked. 'You what?'

"She stopped hanging the sheets and looked straight into my eyes. 'I hate your daddy!' I couldn't speak. 'I have to do something before he kills me or you or one of the other children.'

"'Yessum, Mama,' I said, not sure of what she meant.

"She started to cry, looking at the belt welts all over her and the ones on my arms and legs. 'He almost killed me yesterday, Jeanie. And I see the scars on you and the rest of my girls—and I *hate* him! I can't let him harm my children ever again. Now hand me those clothes. If he sees us talking and not working, he'll swear we're up to something.'

"'Yessum, Mama,' I said.

"Later, he went to those taverns with his old whores and drinking buddies, planning more beatings for us when he got home. After dinner, we sat on the porch with the children and waited. Waited for him to come home."

CHAPTER
18

MURDER

Twenty minutes late, I rushed into Dr. Win's office for my next appointment and settled myself in the recliner. Dr. Win waited for me to get comfortable, then she asked, "How did your father die, Jean?"

Startled, I began breathing more quickly, but managed to reply, "From a gunshot wound. But you know that, Dr. Wintermeyer."

"Yes, dear. I do. I have all your records. Who pulled the trigger?"

My breathing came even more quickly.

"Relax, Jean. Breathe deeply and let yourself relax."

I took several long breaths. "Mama did! You know that too."

She smiled at me comfortingly, "Sometimes it's best if we say things out loud, Jean. 'My mother pulled the trigger. I didn't. My—'"

"My mother? No! It was Mama! Not my mother. Please don't ask me about that now, Dr. Win."

As though she hadn't heard me, she went on. "Did you cry?"

"When he died?" I asked hoarsely.

"Yes." Dr. Win leaned forward.

There was no more to cry about, I thought, then replied, "No! He was dead—we buried him—and I never wept a tear." I was afraid she'd think I was an awful person not to cry over my father's death. I tried to look away, but I couldn't.

She looked me straight in the eyes. "Very good Jean. He was a very mean man. So why should you cry when he died? I can't blame you, Jean. He had tortured your mother for years, beat you and your sisters. He was sadistic, cruel to you! He lived to hurt your mother and you. Your father was a very sick man, Jean. He hurt you a lot."

"I wanted to kill him myself so much." I said. "Seeing him walking up the road, I knew what he'd do to Mama, and to us. I used to run into the cornfield and hide, burying my face in the black dirt. He'd be drunk, staggering; when I got real close to him the nasty smell would gag me."

"Do you still smell that odor when you think of him?"

"It's faded, but it's there."

I began to rock back and forth on the recliner, trying to get away from the scene my mind had conjured up. Dr. Wintermeyer began to speak slowly, soothingly. I felt like I was falling asleep. There was silence.

Then I heard myself begin to speak. "There was a stagnant calmness about that day from the time the sun rose. An ominous feeling clung to the air and seemed stifling. I felt as if I were choking from the dusty crops and heat. The only thing stirring in those dry fields was the gentle sway of green on the corn stalks and high hills of tobacco.

"Mama brushed the perspiration from her face as she washed clothes on her old hand-wringer washer on the front porch in the late morning. We hung them out and watched the hot sun bake them dry. Later we folded the clothes, putting them in a basket as we stood under the clotheslines. We walked back to the house, which seemed so fresh and clean. The floors had been scrubbed for hours with Clorox, the bedding aired, the old stained and rotting mattresses put out on the porch to be aired by the sun."

That beautiful lady, my Mama, was never more pretty than that day. Her high, Indian cheekbones had a sophisticated, chiseled look. Her glossy black hair was pulled neatly back in a bun. I usually followed her every move, but for some reason, I tried not to cling to her apron that day. Something bad was happening to me. I was breathing hard and rapidly. I didn't want Mama to see that. She'd just think it was another "habit" I'd developed. I tried to hold my breath, but it only made me gasp. I felt my heart pounding under my worn and faded blue dress.

"Daddy was dressed in his fine, pink, long-sleeve Sunday dress shirt, starched and ironed by Mama. He also wore his gray gabardine slacks and his felt hat was cocked to the side. He was going to town that afternoon and looked ruggedly handsome.

"I stood watching him from the side of the house. The four-o'clock, Mama's favorite flowers, had just closed their petals for the day. I knew it was time to go inside.

"After supper, late that evening, we all went outside to catch some air on the porch. I still smelled the Clorox from the bleached floors, and the fresh scent filled my senses. From the position I had taken on the porch, I could see the two sweaters Mama had told me to put under the stoop. Sometimes the June air got chilly at night, and I'd caught a cold the last time we ran from him. I could not see the other things Mama had said to hide, but I knew they were there: five or six of Daddy's pocket knives, so he couldn't start pitching them at us in the kitchen, and even some big butcher knives for butchering the hogs."

Mama broke into my thoughts, "Jeanie, did you do all the chores I told you to?"

"Yessum, Mama," I said.

"Gets chilly at night sometimes," she said, as if to herself. "All of them you did, Jeanie?"

"Yessum, Mama. Just like you said."

"You're a good girl, honey. All my youngins are good."

"She started saying how much she missed Dora, her firstborn. Mattie and Beth joined in and hugged her. They told her Dora would come back home one day. That seemed to please her.

"Mama had just turned thirty-three in March and Daddy was thirty-eight that same month, but to me they were my parents and I never saw them as young until I was grown up. It always seems Mama was far older, despite her beautiful face, because of the mere fact that she was Mama.

"Standing at the window, I looked outside. The sun was setting, and cast a reddish glow across Mama's face as she ordered the smaller children to get washed up for bed. A cool dew had fallen on the steps where I sat, my mind was ablaze wondering if this would be the night. I looked at Mama and she looked back at me lingeringly. I would have died and gone to hell for her.

"We put the boys and Beth to bed. Mama allowed me and Mattie to sit with her in the parlor and listen to The

Grand Ole Opry, coming out of Nashville on our favorite radio station, WLAC. We listened to them talk of Hank Williams, who had died several years earlier, as they did each Saturday night. After I'd rocked my brothers and Beth to sleep, I listened to that legendary man's voice. Roy Acuff also sang that night, and as was customary, the Carter Family played. Somewhere during the show, there was always mention of the late and great Jimmy Rogers and his wife. I did not hear that part this night, though. Daddy came home early and Mama switched the radio off before he came inside.

"Her oldest brother, Gordon, brought Daddy home. Mama insisted he join Daddy for a bite of supper. Maybe he saw the desperation in Mama's eyes, because he obliged and talked a lot, trying to keep Daddy calm. I heard Daddy tell him, 'It takes a real man to father all those children in the parlor, and I guess they're mine.'

"'Look just like you and my baby sis,' Uncle Gordon said. 'So you can't deny none of them, R.J. Right pretty youngins, too.' There was silence.

"Then Daddy said, 'Yeah, but they all have a mean streak, just like your sis,' and he went on and on with his complaints. Soon Uncle Gordon got up from the table and went to the back door. 'You don't have to go so soon. Please stay,' Mama begged. But he just got in his truck and left.

"'Where's my boys, Sara?' Daddy yelled out.

"'I have them in bed, R.J.,' she told him. 'I think they woke up with all the noise.'

"'Bring 'em to me, woman. My boys!'

"At Mama's call, the boys came. I saw fear in Will's and Robert's eyes as they passed near me and stepped into the kitchen. Four-year-old Tim was too young to care. That was his daddy, he loved him and he hopped onto his lap. Minutes later Daddy sent them off to bed.

"'You tend' to 'em Jeanie,' he yelled.

"My brief appearance in the kitchen to get the boys sent him into a rage.

"'Damn that blinking your eyes and shaking your head all the time. Are you an idiot?' Miserable, I shook my head.

"I was putting my brothers back to bed when I heard Daddy shouting and cursing at Mama. Mattie and Beth sat on the sofa crying and calling to him, 'Don't hit Mama.' Running to the parlor door, I saw Mama trying to get around him to make it to the back door. He stuck out his legs to trip her, lunging for her. She dodged him and got away, slamming the door. I ran out front and together we got the sweaters and the sack of knives she'd told me to hide. After that, we just kept running till we reached the woods off the main dirt road.

"In the quiet countryside I could still hear Daddy cursing. The girls were calling out for Mama and me. The thing that amazed me was he never beat the children after we ran away. He would fall asleep, maybe in the kitchen or his room or maybe on the porch waiting for us. We never knew where we'd find him when we returned.

"In the pale silver moonlight, Mama and I made our way to a pile of dried pine straw. Here we were hoping to hide and find safety till Mama decided when to go home. She helped me put on my old sweater. When I saw she was softly weeping, I wiped the tears from her face. She held me close and kissed my face gently as she spoke.

"'May God forgive me for what I will do tonight,' she

choked. 'If my Maker spares my life, I will kill your daddy before the sun rises.'

"'I'll shoot him, Mama!' I managed to whisper. 'Then you won't have to. Please, Mama! Let me kill him.'

"'Ssshhh, Jeanie,' she said. 'Rest now on my shoulder for a little while. We have to leave very soon.'

"'Yessum, Mama.'

"'We'll leave the woods and walk down the road about a quarter of a mile and spend the time we need resting in our neighbor's house.'

"I fell asleep. I wasn't aware of the hour when Mama woke me. We began the short walk. Our neighbors, the Stevens, were wonderful country folks. Well off and deeply religious, they welcomed us each time. Their house was dark. The animals in the stalls were silent. The couple were at least in their sixties, and they had an old maid daughter, Elvie, who was in her late forties. It was Miss Elvie who answered our knocking on the door.

"'Lord no, Sara!' Miss Elvie gasped. 'You can't go on like this. R.J. has to stop beatin' you, woman. Did you take out the peace bond like Ma and Pa told you?'

"I looked shocked. I knew nothing of any peace bond till that moment. 'Yes, Elvie,' Mama said as Elvie showed us to the guest bedroom. 'Over a month back I took it out. Took me forever to get ten dollars.'

"'And what did Magistrate Martin have to say, Sara?'

"'Said I oughta leave R.J. before he kills me or one of the children or all of us.'

"'Did you tell him?' Elvie asked.

"Mama was nervous. 'No. I was too scared to tell him, Elvie. Can me and Jeanie wash off our feet and rest a while in the bed? I'm real tired.'

"'Of course you can, Sara. Now what in God's name good is a ten-dollar peace bond if you still—'

"'Not now, Elvie, I'm nearly droppin' I'm so tired.'

"Miss Elvie produced a wash basin and cloths, not rags like we had at our house, and we washed our feet spotless. Quickly, we got into bed. The sheets were so soft and to my surprise there were no holes in them. I fell asleep in no time. It was a light sleep; I was aware that Mama was lying beside me and breathing heavily. It seemed no matter how weary she was, she couldn't sleep. I was afraid I would have nightmares and say things the Stevens' family might hear, but I didn't. I slept peacefully.

"It seemed like hours later when Mama woke me. The clock on the night stand said 1:25 A.M. As I crawled out of the warm and comfortable bed, Mama put her finger to her lips. 'Don't make noise. I don't want to awaken Miss Elvie.'

"I followed her example . We eased out of the house, closing and locking the door behind us.

"The moon seemed much brighter. I could make out the shadows and silhouettes of crops in the field ready for harvesting, and barns, old and lopsided, looming in the darkness. Dogs howled far off in the distance. It was the loneliest sound I'd ever heard. I clung to Mama's hand as we walked up the road, we kept to the edge behind the tall bushes in case Daddy was waiting for us along the way.

"'You think Mattie unlocked the door, Mama?' I whispered.

"'Yes, Jeanie,' she said. 'If your daddy fell asleep first, she did.'

"She squeezed my hand and told me to be quiet. 'I took the shells out we're going to need, honey! Trust

Mama! Today when R.J. left for town, I took them out. They're in the outhouse on the shelf, behind a paint can.

"'You'll have to get them when I say it's time. Don't talk now, we're too close to home.' she whispered. We made sure we walked in back under the pecan trees to reach the yard. It seemed as if even the dirt was my enemy. My feet were afraid to take each step, as if dynamite was set to explode if I did.

"We had reached the back door. Mama put her hand on the old, white round knob. It turned. I was right behind her as she put her foot on the steps. She turned to see my face.

"'No!' she breathed, so low I barely heard her. 'Go get the box of shells. Hurry, Jeanie. He might be awake.'

"She stood guard at the door while I ran to the outhouse. I fumbled in the dark, groping around and then clutching the box. I held the shells tightly in my hands, gathering them to my chest as if Mama's and my life depended on them. Indeed they did. Trembling, I made my way to the door and handed the box to her.

"Standing in the doorway, I watched while Mama loaded the gun. She nodded. 'The chamber is ready,' she murmured. She inspected the trigger and safety to make sure they were in working order. Everything was happening within two or three minutes, but it seemed forever since we entered the yard.

"Mama took a step inside. I tried to follow. She shook her head back and forth, gesturing for me to stay seated on the steps. I did as Mama said.

"She moved through the kitchen stealthily. I never even heard the old floors squeak that night. They always squeaked, waking us when someone was up. Maybe I was dreaming, I told myself, asleep and having a nightmare.

"I stared at the ground, my head bent down. Even my breaths came slowly, hanging in the air. Not really knowing what I was waiting for, I dug my fingernails into my palms. Nothing seemed real. No sounds came from the shack. Never had it seemed so silent, even though dogs were still howling in the distance. A million thoughts, but none of substance, passed through my mind. My heart beat fast and furiously.

"Suddenly, a shot rang out! I sat frozen for a second, the longest second of my life. I didn't think. I couldn't think. The sound of that shot filled my senses and engulfed my entire being, as if I were suspended in a place where there were no other sounds. No sounds of life. Just the horrifying sound of a shot signifying death.

"An eternity seemed to pass before Mama ran outside and towards me. She grabbed my hand and dragged me from the steps, around to the side of the house.

"'Is he dead, Mama?' I asked over and over. 'Tell me! Is he dead?'

"'Hush, Jeanie! I think so, but I'm not sure. I shot him once. You have to help me now.'

"'What, Mama? What have I got to do?'

"'Oh, God, no!' She was holding— 'No! I won't do that! I can't! NO! NO'

Through the haze of the past, I could hear the soft voice of Dr. Wintermeyer.

"Slow your breathing down, Jeanie. What is she trying to make you do?"

My head jerked back against the chair. My heart pounded. My body trembled. I had to leave that room!

"Nothing," I said. "She ain't making me do anything.

I want to stop now. I can't bear it in here, Dr. Wintermeyer."

"Jeanie, you can stop any time you feel like it. I can see you're in pain, but it would be better to let all this come out. What is she—?"

The past claimed me again. "No, Mama! Please don't make me do that."

"Do what, Jeanie?" Dr. Win asked.

I was crying uncontrollably. "I done all the things you told me to—so please, Mama! I'm a good girl. I always do what you tell me. I'm sorry for all the habits I got, Mama, but please, I can't—"

"Listen to your voice Jean," Dr. Wintermeyer said softly. "Listen and hear how it sounds."

"No, Mama! NO! NO! NO! I won't."

Dr. Win's voice broke in. "You aren't Jean now, dear. You're Jeanie. The child who was abused. Hear your voice. It sounds like that of a little girl. Now tell me—let Jeanie tell me what your Mama wants you to do. You can make it through this. I'm here with you."

Still mixing the past and the present, I responded, "But I can't stop crying. Mama's making me try to stop—but I can't. It hurts so bad! How could Mama—I love you, Mama! Don't hand me that, I hate that thing!"

"What, Jean?" Dr. Wintermeyer said. "What is she trying to make you take? Look in her hand. What is she holding? What, Jean?"

"It's his—" I began hyperventilating and couldn't stop. "It's Daddy's—the—No, Mama! I kept our secrets, I done all you—No they won't, Mama! They know he beats you! They won't make you go to jail if—yessum, Mama. I always mind you. I'm a good girl. Yes ma'am, Mama. I will.

I'll do anything for you, Mama. I'd die for you, Mama. Don't hate me for doing it, though, Mama. Please don't. But I will."

"You're so close," Dr. Win said, "Keep on, Jeanie. Go on and do what it is your Mama said to. Take the object she's offering you. Take it, Jeanie."

"I can see it! I feel it. I hate it."

"What does if feel like, Jeanie?"

"It's leather."

"What is it? What does she want you to do with it?"

"It's leather! It's a leather belt—one of Daddy's leather belts! Please! I can't do—yessum, I will!"

"What are you doing now, Jean?" Dr. Wintermeyer asked. "Why does your Mama want you to take the belt?"

My body shook wildly against the back of the reclined chair. I was desperately gasping for air. I could no longer hear my doctor speaking to me. In my mind I was in the past again, at the side of the house by the bedroom window where my three brothers slept. I had the belt in my hand.

"'Do it, Jeanie!' Mama ordered me. 'You have to beat me with the belt!'

"'No!'

"'I will go to jail otherwise. You have to put scars on me. Make welts, Jeanie. Now! We have to hurry! Beat me, Jeanie!'

"And so I did.

"Mama lifted her faded blouse high around her neck. I saw her delicate hands let it slide up her back. I saw the white of her skin in the moonlight. Her long black hair had come undone. It hung down against her shoulders. She lifted it up, too.

"Taking a deep trembling breath, I drew back and swung. The belt hit her side. I took another and another. 'Beat me harder,' she cried. And I did! Whatever Mama asked, I always did. I was a good girl. The belt zoomed up behind me, gaining power as I swung it hard against her back.

"'Again,' she said.

"I hit her over and over. Red welts had begun to appear on her back. The belt seemed to have a mind and power all its own. I was crying as I beat Mama. I told myself it was a nightmare from which I'd soon awaken. No one who had beat their Mama with a leather belt should be allowed to live, so of course it was a horrible dream—except for once I could not run and hide in a closet or plug my ears to drown out Mama's cries of pain. Or the pain I felt each time the belt hit her.

"Mama finally stopped the belt in midair and, crying, said, 'That's enough, Jeanie. Let's go inside and get the children. Hurry. He might not be dead.'

"Mama pulled her blouse down and started walking around the house, but I couldn't move. I felt rooted to the dirt and prayed I would wake up. A noise behind me brought me back to some sort of reality. I looked around, and my God! There was my brother Robert tapping on the window pane and staring at me! Seeing all I had done. Watching me beat our Mama. He never spoke a word, as if he wanted it to be a dream also.

"Poor Robert. Poor, dear Robert. My oldest little brother. We didn't know then what that night, the murder of the father who'd tortured him, and then the horrible scene of his sister, beating our Mama, did to him inside."

My screams echoed in the room. Unable to stop

them or go on, I sobbed hysterically while Dr. Wintermeyer held me. Suddenly, I couldn't stand it any more. I broke from her hold and ran to the bathroom. I was gagging. Never had I felt so sick, sick to my guts. I wretched, but nothing came up, just that awful sound of gagging. I put three fingers in my mouth and gagged and gagged.

I was on my knees, my head bowed down to the toilet. The nauseated sickness came forth in waves as if purging Jeanie Small from my system. Finally, hot, sticky water and food emptied from deep inside me. It poured out till there was nothing left in me but the lining of my stomach. I threw up everything that was in me, all the nasty horrors that had dwelled in my soul for all my adult life and most of my childhood.

Finally, I got up and washed my face with a cold cloth, wiping the inside of my mouth and teeth. Slowly, I began walking back into the doctor's office. I knew Dr. Wintermeyer assumed I had gone into the bedroom that night and discovered Daddy was killed. She didn't imagine that I had aided Mama in his death and then had been forced to beat Mama with a leather belt. I hoped she'd understand. I walked inside.

"Are you all right, Jeanie?" Dr. Wintermeyer asked compassionately. "Can you drive yourself home, or shall I call Gary or Monty?"

"I think I'm okay. I'll make it home by myself if I have to crawl," I told her. "I'll do it alone, maybe for the first time."

She smiled her voice was gentle, "I'm glad, Jeanie."

"I can do it."

"I know you can," she said.

Now I just wanted to get outside and feel the chill of that autumn day against my face. I wanted to feel it cleanse my body, mind and soul. I had relived the pain of my father's death, the belt striking Mama, the pain for her and for Jeanie, the child who was part of me. For the first time, I had confronted my "sin," that is what I deemed to be the sin of little Jeanie. I had felt it and faced it. It had been at the root of an illness I still didn't completely understand. But now I knew it wasn't my sin. It wasn't Mama's. It was nobody's. It was the tragedy of that long ago life. The childhood life of Jeanie Small.

Once outside, I sat in the car for a while, just feeling the warmth of the sun and thinking. The rest of that awful time passed in front of me like a collection of snapshots, some old and faded, some too real to comprehend.

I was in the funeral home standing over Daddy's casket, looking down at his face. He wore a black suit with a white shirt and he looked so healthy and tanned. I had heard that if you touched a dead person, you'd never have nightmares about them. Slowly, I reached out my right hand and let it rest on his forehead. It was hard and cold to the touch even in the heat of the parlor. His cheekbones seemed to rise even higher, in death, and I imagined his deep blue eyes staring at me.

Then all my brothers, sisters and I were sitting in a circle around the gravesite. Uncles, aunts and cousins stared at us, especially me. I had taken Mama's position like I was the little wife. I had been seated closest to the casket. It was draped with the American flag and flowers.

Someone began removing the wreath from on top and men started taking off the flag and folding it in some strange fashion I'd never seen. They were friends of

Daddy's, veterans, but not in uniform. His sister had wanted a full military service with the guns fired and casket saluted. Mama was outraged at such an idea, "No! I will not allow it!," she said. The neatly folded flag was presented to me, laid in my lap, and I didn't even know why or what to do with it, so I held on to it.

During the funeral, Mama was at her sister's, heavily sedated and under a doctor's care. She was out of jail after one night, on a one thousand dollar bond posted by our landlord. I later handed the flag to her and she put it in a drawer, as if she were ashamed of it having been involved in a death such as Daddy's.

Maybe, just maybe, I thought, all the pieces of my life, past and present, had finally come together. I knew this was the only way I could begin to heal, to understand the torment and the love which was my childhood. I had to see that time as it really was—grotesque but real. Now I could allow it to exist. Not just Mama and child, but Daddy and child, forever—even in death. The thought did not frighten me; rather, it warmed my soul.

CHAPTER
19

BREAKTHROUGH

"Don't hide now, Jean." Dr. Win hugged me and said, "Let Jeanie drift back in your mind. Just try to be a woman facing her life in the proper perspective."

After some time, she moved to a nearby chair and spoke gently to me.

"Don't lose this now, Jean. You've been such a great patient—helping me to help you. You've made great efforts and they've paid off. In my sessions with Gary and your sons, they praised you the whole time. You're not out of control anymore. You ask something of Gary, rather than demand it. I've never worked with a family who loved and cared for each other more than you, Shane, Monty and Gary."

"I don't deserve them, Dr. Win," I cried.

"Yes you do, Jean. But first you've got to learn to live with the past, accept it and move forward. Then you have to forgive yourself, and then they'll forgive you."

I wiped my tear-filled eyes and tried to keep from sobbing as I looked at her. "Dr. Win, do you know what it's like to wake up every day and not know who you are, or what you'll do to yourself before the day's over? Who you'll hurt?"

"Obsessive-compulsive behavior, Jean. It began in your tortured childhood, and because you never worked through those awful memories—some of which caused nightmares, some of which you buried, some of which caused you to develop other personalities—continued all your life.

"I feel like I can't go on! I will lose my mind. My body is worn out. The smelling, the cleaning, the clothes-folding, I hate it! Won't I ever be normal?"

"If what you mean by 'normal' is the same as those people who have not had these experiences or somehow seem not to be injured by them, then no, Jean. You will never be that kind of 'normal.'"

That angered me. "Then what will I be, Dr. Win? A woman on the verge of insanity all my life, a crazy bitch? I can't go on like this!"

"But you must, Jean. This craziness is a part of your life. Because of the past and the way it's affected you, you've developed these personality disorders. Do you understand?"

"I do. They aren't gelled—aren't one person."

"They're fragments of many people. The child Jeanie who hides in closets to free herself of pain and fear. The mean woman who curses at her family and acts out her anger and fear. And the decent woman who is loving and kind." She shifted in her chair, putting her face closer to mine. "Don't you see Jean? In different ways, we're all Dr.

Jekylls and Mr. Hydes. It's just that you began as an abused child—little Jeanie—separating into other parts of your personality. You yearned to be 'normal,' but you couldn't resolve your conflicts. Most of us deal with our problems, but yours run so deep you couldn't without wanting to commit suicide. But now you are becoming able to deal with your past."

I nodded, "I don't think of killing myself anymore. But at times, I dwell on death because it offers me a peace I've never had."

"Most of us think of death, especially when we're in emotional and physical pain. If your time comes, let it be God who takes you. He gave you life, give him the honor of taking it."

Dr. Win always taped our sessions when I entered the "room," and she always offered to let me hear them, but only in her presence. It took me a long time to be able to listen to all the pain I expressed. When I did, I gained much faith, not only in her as my doctor, but in myself and my ability to live with my past and my ability to try to change certain things about myself. I tried to accept that I would never be "normal" in the broad sense, that my abnormality was my normal behavior.

Now I had to learn not to take those abnormalities beyond the limit she referred to as, "within the realm of sanity," but accept and know them in moderation. She explained that my obsessive-compulsive behavior was born out of the horror of my childhood during which I longed to be perfect like my Mama. And all the clothes I'd torn off my body because of the holes, I'd done so to destroy anything with "flaws." Things or people with "flaws" were dirty. I wanted them out of my life. I was compelled to rid myself of them.

"We know so little about obsessive-compulsive behavior," she said sadly. "We're just now putting a name to it and are still trying to develop therapy and medications for patients like you. We do know it is caused by a chemical imbalance in the brain, but the question is, what activates the behavior. In your case, it started with your daddy and the pain he caused you. Afterwards, since you never really understood or dealt with the pain you felt, you could not get rid of the behavior. Some patterns you may never be able to rid yourself of. Nevertheless, you can gain control when they leap out of bounds.

"If you try to smooth every wrinkle out of every sheet and piece of clothing, you'll never succeed, Jean, and you'll only make yourself more frustrated. If you try to vacuum all the dirt, pick up all the lint, scrub every crevice in the floor, polish each piece of furniture each time it has dust, wash the walls beside the stove where the grease splatters, or do the laundry as soon as it hits the hamper, you'll fail, Jean. Life is full of flaws—we as people are full of flaws and that makes us human, not perfect. Take away the flaws and you remove our individuality, our personality, the parts of us that give us the freedom to be ourselves. You can't make things or people perfect, dear."

"And you think I try to do that, Dr. Win?" I asked.

"Yes. Your mother isn't perfect. I'll bet she never said she was. But you thought she was, so therefore, you tried to be perfect for her. You failed because no human being is perfect. So what if your sisters think she's an angel? Don't let that concern you, Jean. Your mother knows she isn't. Concentrate on your relationship with her and try to be yourself around her. Try to see her as 'Mama,' the one you knew on the farm. They're the same person."

I became livid. "No! Don't ever say that, Dr. Win. Mama was my perfect angel, but I don't know 'Mother.' I'm not sure I want to know her." I was chain-smoking, realizing I had allowed the anger I tried to keep within me to surface again, to push me out of control. "And why did you let me stay in the 'room' today? Why did you hurt me like that? I've never been afraid of the room before. It was mine and it was a safe place for me to go and sort things out—even at home. Now you've destroyed that! I want to know why you allowed me to stay in there and live through that hell? Why, Dr. Win?"

She walked over to put the tape on rewind. "Would you like to hear it today?"

"I never want to hear that one, destroy it!"

"Very well, dear." She quickly removed the tape and started pulling it from its cartridge, the two spools flying in the air as she pulled the tape off and wadded it in her hands. Forming a ball she tossed it into the trash. "There. You feel better now, Jean?"

"I will. Give me time!" I snapped. We had never had become angry with each other and I could see she was frustrated with me. "You had no right, Dr. Win, to hurt me in the room."

"If you really believe I hurt you in that room, then get up and walk out, Jean. Because you're wasting my time. And I don't waste time on any patient."

"What's the matter, Dr. Win? Did I hit a nerve? Did I hit a flaw in you—the perfect therapist? The woman who's so damn religious she doesn't believe in a damn and hell? A flaw in Miss God Almighty herself?"

"You've come too far, Jean. I won't allow you to destroy what you've accomplished. You can't give up and retreat into mental illness again as if it were a place where you could be safe."

Dr. Win paused and her voice hardened.

"Walk away dear, if you don't want to hear the truth. Go now and save me some time. Get out, Mrs. Brinson."

"Don't call me that, you hateful woman! You want to drive me crazy!"

"You are Mrs. Brinson right now!" she shouted at me. "So tell me, where's Jeanie the saddest child on earth? Did she abandon you? Did she run off and leave you?"

"No, no. She'll always be here with me. Why are you—"

"How many asylums, Mrs. Brinson? Five? Six? How many times have you tried to commit suicide? Rat poison, carbon monoxide, valium, more rat poison? God, how you must hate yourself!"

I slumped down in the chair wishing I could slide through the floorboards.

"Being in an asylum made you feel like you'd escaped. In a way you had. As long as you could be insane, you didn't have to face reality—the real world like your husband and sons face every day. You could stay in bed for days, hide in closets when the fear and insanity caught up with you—but tell me, Mrs. Brinson," she brought her face within an inch of mine, "where could Gary, Shane and Monty hide? What was their safe place? They couldn't, they have had to face reality and so do you."

Dr. Win paced the floor and was speaking now in low tones, almost a whisper. "Perhaps it wasn't that the therapists you saw were incompetent. You never cared enough to allow anyone to help you. You get sick, stay in deep depressions for weeks, try to kill yourself and end up in crazy houses. When you'd take too many pills, you'd lie in bed nearly dead. Gary and the boys would sit by you to watch over you all night. They were always there for you—but where were you when they needed a mother? A wife?"

"I tried to be a wife. I tried so hard. You have to believe the truth, Dr. Win. But Gary wouldn't stop drinking and I—"

"You saw him as your daddy, Mrs. Brinson," she said.

"I don't know. I was sick long before I met Gary," I told her. "But it got worse—and the baby came and I was afraid I'd hurt my baby."

"Jean, you must try to understand. What you had was postpartum depression. It is an illness, an illness you overcame when you didn't hurt your child and learned you had strength."

"I just wanted peace—that's all I ever wanted. I never meant to hurt Gary and the boys! I love them, they're my life!"

"The only life you have had since your father's death is one in which you walked a tightrope. At the far pole was sanity, but if you fell off as you tried to maintain your balance, you careened into a world of illusions, guilt and hate for yourself and the world where you couldn't bear the truth, or face the fear and pain."

I shook my head wildly. "That's not true, Dr. Win."

"Sure it is. You blame anyone and everyone for your problems. You blame me for the torment you felt today in the room. But I didn't do that to you, Mrs. Brinson." She was standing close, looking down at my trembling body. "You did that to yourself. I told you, Mrs. Brinson, no one could ever enter your room unless you allowed them. It is your place, your secret place to learn about *you*. You could have opened your eyes and walked up the stairs at any moment, Jean. You remained in the room because you wanted to feel the pain—to live it and tell it goodbye forever."

"I started seeing things I didn't like."

"You wanted help, Jean," she told me. "That's why you stayed. You wanted to see the truth."

"But I feel I always knew."

"Knowing in some far recess of your mind and actually facing it is not the same. Today you faced reality for the first time—the bitter truth that you helped your Mama carry out her plan for the murder of your own father."

"I was just a child, for God's sake, Dr. Win." I said. "I did what I was told. I'd have died for my Mama. Nobody on earth seems to see how much she meant to me. She was my whole life. I was a good girl, always good for Mama."

Dr. Wintermeyer took my trembling hands in hers. "Yes, you were. You were the best girl a mother could want, but you were a child, Jean. I want you to say it. Say it over and over until you can realize and accept the fact you did as you were told because that was all you knew how to do."

"But I wanted to help my Mama," I wept. "I begged her to let me shoot him. I'm not sorry I helped her murder him."

She patted my hand like I was a lost child. "I know, but you have to remember you were a child. Say it, Jean! Say it! As your doctor I'm asking you to say it. 'I was a child. I was just a child. A good girl for Mama—but still a child.'"

I began nodding my head rapidly. "Yes, yes. I am—I was a child, a little girl."

"Say it. 'I am an individual. I am not my mother or my mama. I am not any of my sisters or brothers no matter how much I love them. I don't have to be like them to be normal. I am me—Jean Small Brinson.'"

I began slowly repeating each word she had said, holding onto it as if fresh air were starting to flow inside me. Dr. Win rose and paced the room, speaking gently yet with authority to this woman-child in such pain.

"Say it, Jean. Say it a thousand times until you see and believe it in your soul. 'I was a child! I was a child, Mama!'"

I did as she told me. "'I was a child! I was a child. But I love you, Mama, and I did it for you. I was a child! I was!'"

She reached over and held my hands in hers. "Don't you see now, Jean? You didn't get the answers to anything in the room today that you didn't already have. You looked it in the face, saw reality for the first time, and it caused you great pain. I told you from the start of our working together—you will never see or hear anything in that room that you don't already know.

"However, it may be caught beneath the surface or deep in your subconscious. Now it has all come out. But it's not the same, Jean. For the first time all the different parts of you, little Jeanie, Jean and Mrs. Brinson know. More importantly, even though you helped your mama carry out your father's death and the beating, you were just a child obeying orders."

"Dr. Win, I don't like to think of myself with all of these people and parts inside me. It makes me feel sicker."

"Dear, you have a personality disorder. You aren't like the woman in 'Three Faces of Eve' who has split into many persons. It might be easier if you were. Instead, you're bits and pieces and fragments of different personalities. When you can't bear the pain of life, you become Jeanie Small. When you're angry at the entire world and hate everything, you become Mrs. Brinson and try to kill yourself. When you are happy, you become Jean the good wife and mother."

"Jean is a good person, isn't she, Dr. Win?"

She half smiled. "Yes. She is the closest thing to 'normal' that you have ever been, Jean. You can learn to live with the flaws you have, take the good and make the most of it, or you can succumb to a life of insanity. Worse yet, you can succumb to being what you've been all you life—somewhere between sane and insane. Do you see that, Jean?"

I nodded. "Change what I can, accept what I can't, and the wisdom to know the difference. Isn't that the way it goes?"

She nodded. "More or less."

I was preparing to get my purse to leave. Neither of us was talking much. Dr. Win was writing the date of my next session in her appointment book .

"I don't think I can come back—not for a long time," I told her.

"Why not, dear?"

"I can't ever go to the room again. I'll live in fear of it now. It was my safe place to go, to learn things about me, to help me and my sons and Gary. Now it means just another place to get hurt. I'm tired of hurting."

She handed me my appointment card. "You'll enter the room again, Jean. Not because I want you to, but because you have to. You can't stop now. You won't allow yourself. Not till you have all the answers you can find."

"But we know everything, Dr. Win," I said.

"No, Jean. If we did, we wouldn't be having this discussion. There's something else in that room, and you won't stop until you face it."

THE INQUEST

It was our very next session. I was back in the "room" and heard myself speaking. "Afterward, we got the children out of bed and ran to a neighbor's farmhouse since nobody around there had a phone. Our neighbor drove Mama to get the magistrate so she could tell him what had happened. Later the sheriff came and took Mama to the Conway County Jail. Mama stayed in jail just that one night. Her thousand-dollar bond was posted by our landowner and his wife. Later she would tell me it was the most peaceful night's sleep she'd had since marrying my daddy.

"When the day of the inquest arrived, we slowly dressed for court. I put on the best dress I had, white cotton with flowers on it. Mama had made it for me. Mama wore a navy blue silklike dress that she'd used when she was last pregnant over four years past. It had giant white polka dots, and Mama tied a white sash around her tiny waist, so no one would know it was a maternity dress.

"As we walked in, I looked wide-eyed around the courthouse. Every seat was filled. People stood in the rear and outside on the steps and lawn. Friends of mine from school, girls, boys and their parents, everyone from my church was there. I wasn't scared anymore though, I just felt shame that now they would all know that my daddy beat us. We'd kept it a secret for so long. Now I had no refuge, no place to hide. Looking around, I thought it was the largest court room in the world. I felt like it was going to consume me, swallow me like a morsel of food.

"As we huddled together, it was Mama, Mattie and me against twelve white men who would decide if she were to be indicted. My older sister, Dora, was still living in Florida and hadn't come home for the funeral or inquest. My sisters and I were instructed by the judge to look at the twelve jurors and tell them our story about Daddy's brutality from the time we could remember. Mattie went first. She was just twelve and I felt so sorry for her. Mattie stuttered through her testimony. She had stuttered all her life, but that disappeared when she was older and no longer had to live in fear of Daddy. Then it was my turn. As I told my story, I saw women weeping in the audience. When I was almost finished, my Aunt Caroline, Daddy's sister, stood up.

"She began cursing at Mama. The judge ordered her to sit down or be ejected. She never forgave Mama, nor did Daddy's other sister and one brother.

"Then he dismissed the jury. I sat behind Mama, waiting for her fate to be revealed.

"Finally the jury came out. I knew one of the men, since it so happened it was his home Mama and I had run to the night Daddy was killed. I looked in his eyes and the only thing I could see was kindness. All the others had known Mama or her daddy all their lives. I began to pray.

"Finally the chairman of the jury spoke.

"'We, the jury, find that Mrs. Small acted in self-defense, Your Honor,' he said decisively. 'Having gone through what this woman did for seventeen years, we believe she feared for her life. We feel she had no choice but to wait until her husband was sleeping and shoot him. He would have killed her if he'd been awake. It is for those reasons, Your Honor, we cannot in all fair conscience and guidance indict Mrs. Small.'

"'Your verdict is not guilty due to self-defense?'" the judge asked.

"'It is, Your Honor, and we are all so agreed.'

"Mama and we children stayed on the tobacco farm until the next year and after that, unable to make enough money to live, we moved to Charleston."

Dr. Win brought me out of my dreamlike state. I sat upright, tears running down my face. I was crying uncontrollably. Dr. Win had torn my guts out this time. I think she wanted me to say something, maybe tell her I hated her for it, but I couldn't.

She had brought me out of the "room" now, and still I couldn't get control of myself. I rubbed my hand together harshly until they were wringing with sweat, then I swung my arms wildly beside the chair. She gave me a perfumed tissue which I couldn't stop tapping on my nose as I was counting to myself—one, two, three—no! One, two, three, four, five. The sweet scent of the tissue was making me sick. I opened and shut my eyes quickly, over and over. At the same time I began nodding my head. Dr. Win watched closely as I picked lint from my clothes and picked at the chair. After that I started having chills. Dr. Win got a blanket, wrapped it around me and held me close to her as a mother would her lost child. Though I could not see her through the tears in my own eyes, I sensed she was weeping. In an instant I became the child Jeanie, afraid and sad.

I had to get out of Dr. Win's office. Hurriedly, I said good-bye, gathered my things and rushed out the door.

21

THE LONG
RIDE HOME

I ran to my car, opened the door, threw my purse on the seat and strapped myself in. Now I was safe. Safe, that is, if I sat there in Dr. Win's parking lot the rest of my life. I knew that wasn't practical or even possible. I had to get home. Gary would be worried, think I'd done something to hurt myself. I cranked up the car, slowly pushing down the gas pedal, and almost glided to the main highway. I saw cars coming in every direction and a cold fear was settling in my guts. Blindly, I eased out onto the four lane interstate highway and was immediately propelled into a world of frenzied fear, gasping and choking simultaneously.

I had to find an offramp. I had to get off that massive highway. If I didn't—oh, God. I'd lose all control of my actions and slam my car into—no. I couldn't allow myself to think that. My palms were so sweaty, they stuck to the steering wheel. I took the belt from my skirt and tied it around my left hand, leaving free only my right to steer with. The belt was wrapped around my wrist several times and tied to the steering wheel. My face was on fire. By this time, there wasn't one inch of my body that was not shaking and out of control.

I kept talking to myself: "You know this place, you've been on this road many times. Try to relax." Finally I saw an offramp that read, "Visitors Information Center." I pulled off. Though it was late in the afternoon, it was still bright daylight on that early June day. But to my horror, the information center was closed. I pulled the car around back and was going to park and pray the attack would subside, but then I saw arrows pointing to a secondary road. I drove toward it. There were no cars; I was in luck. I pulled onto the other road and drove slowly, trying to look for something familiar.

About half a mile up the road I saw a large pond. It was a place where Gary and I took the boys every year for an outing. I drove toward the site I remembered and followed the signs until I was parked by the pond. There were several children and parents walking along the sidewalk that bordered the pond. If I could just ask them for help. I told myself I had to. But what would they think—I was insane? Maybe they'd be right. Maybe this was it, the day I finally stepped over the edge of sanity and I'd never return to any kind of normal life. Maybe being in the "room" that day, seeing and realizing and fully accepting the fact that I had helped Mama with Daddy's murder, maybe that was the final trauma.

The pond was in front of me. I couldn't bear looking at the water. My mind spun backwards to when I was a child riding in Daddy's open wagon while he beat the mules to go faster. Around and around the curves and bends he flew. He cracked the whip against the mules' hide and they neighed in terror while I hid in the wagon and buried my face in my hands, often pulling my ragged dress over my eyes to shut out the world around me. I knew that at any moment the wagon could turn over and throw me off into the trees.

I had the same feeling of fear now. Slowly, I drove the car to the farthest end of the pond away from people and the main highway. I parked as far away from the water as I could, on the grass where signs were posted saying *not* to park. I was worn out. I got a Valium from my purse and used my saliva to swallow since I had nothing to drink. Then I took out a pack of cigarettes and began smoking. I'd eaten no lunch and I was becoming nauseated, but nothing mattered. Nothing but the fear, cold and misery that gnawed at my brain till I was unable to think rationally.

I lay across the seats, trembling, and prayed the feeling would pass. "God help me." I prayed, "Let me die or have peace and remove all my fears." There was no answer. "I gave him so many choices," I mumbled. "Why couldn't He answer my begging?" I tried to relax, to let the tranquilizer work. Even if the attack passed, I was far too weak to drive. I hated myself for being so weak as to base my hopes on a small yellow pill instead of taking control of my life for myself.

The late-day sun streamed in on my face. Already the skyline was growing darker. I drifted in and out of sleep. Once again I saw my daddy. I relived every second of the day of his death.

Then it was another point in time, two weeks later. We were sweeping the yards with sweet gum branches dried to make yard brooms. Since there was no grass on the ground, every inch was swept clean as if it were our parlor. I could see little Jeanie and Mattie sweeping throughout the day.

Then it was another time—I think sometime before the night he was actually killed. I could hear him in the parlor beating Mama, her cries filling my ears. I was overcome with fear. I couldn't bear it! I ran to the outhouse as I often did and stood in the corner with my head buried in my hands. The stench was unbearable! I saw maggots and worms and could feel them crawling all over me. I started crying and pulling fistfuls of my stringy, dishwater blond hair. Still I couldn't make the bugs stop crawling over me. I ran from the outhouse, trying to get the maggots off of me and drown out Mama's cries and screams.

Then I was at the tobacco barn and there were men working and gathering drag loads of the green sticky leaves, tying it onto sticks with twine. I was handing it to a black woman from one side and Mattie on the other side and I couldn't do it right because I couldn't make Mama's screams of torment go away. Daddy was in the old shack beating her with the belt.

When I couldn't bear it another second, I ran towards the house, but this giant man, a grin on his face, stopped me, saying, "let the man take care of his old lady." I ran into the woods, out of control, tearing my dress from my body. I tore it to shreds. I was there all alone in my step-ins. I tried to wrap the rags and tie them around my body just until I could get inside the house, but they fell off. Finally, right after sunset, I sneaked in through an open window and got dressed again.

"Why?" I asked myself, "Why is my mind running over with thoughts of my anguished childhood? Other children had survived physical abuse, why can't I get over it?"

I felt guilty about the suicide attempts and the cruelty my tortured self had inflicted on those I loved most. However, what tormented me the most was my weakness. I couldn't stop being obsessive. All my phobias had come full circle now, coming to a head like a deadly spider bite. No phobia was independent of the other; rather, they appeared together in rapid response to the initial attack on me, like delayed harbingers of my childhood of abuse.

When I finally woke up it was dark. No one was at the pond. Still petrified, but knowing I had to go to my family, I slowly drove away from the pond and started home. I took all the secondary roads, so it seemed to take forever as I battled myself, the elements and my attack, which only ceased when I reached our driveway. Gary, Monty and Shane came running from the porch where they'd been waiting. Gary jerked on the car door till I unlocked it.

"Jean! My God, Jean! Where've you been, honey?" He started. Then he looked at me closely. "You look sick."

I was crying and could barely speak as I tried to explain about the attack and how I'd fallen asleep after taking a Valium. The boys were hugging me and crying.

"I thought you tried to kill yourself again, Mom," Shane said. "You didn't, did you, Mom? You didn't take pills or poison?"

"No, sweetie," I managed. "Mom just had an intense panic attack. I had to pull off the highway; it was—oh, God! I was never so scared, Gary."

They helped me into the house. I slumped down into a chair in the kitchen. All of them were talking at once, saying how much they loved me and how worried they'd been. I kept kissing my husband's and my sons' precious faces, holding each of them tightly against me.

It had been nearly six months since my therapy began with Dr. Wintermeyer, and as we sat there loving one another, respecting each others' feelings and opinions, I realized I'd come a long way. For the first time in years, I felt a part of my family unit. That day of therapy, especially, but also many other ones, had been excruciating. Now, as I held my husband and children, feeling their love for me, I decided that even my trips to the "room" were worth it.

At last, I had a reason to do whatever it took to get better. In fact, I had three special reasons. "I promise you and God this night," I said, "since we four have been through so much pain and sadness, I will not stop until all the murderous memories are removed from Jean Brinson's mind, and I am as close to the mother and wife you deserve."

EPILOGUE

My sessions continued with Dr. Wintermeyer for just over two more years. I've never met a more caring and loving person or a better therapist. I do not stay in touch with her, though. For me, it would be too painful. I will forever owe her much of my sanity.

My therapy with Dr. Wintermeyer greatly increased my self-knowledge: I discovered it's all right if I smell the sheets and hang up all the clothes in the same order in the closet. It's okay if I match up all the lines and stripes in sheets and clothing. It's okay if I brush my teeth for thirty minutes and wash my face that long. It's okay if I pick lint from my clothes continually and scrub the sinks many times a day. It's okay if I count to three or five or a thousand, if I want to. If I have to turn off the light several times, so what? All these obsessive-compulsive behaviors are okay as long as I am in control of them and know when to stop for the sake of my sanity. As well as some virtues, it is all those flaws that make up the character of

Jean Small Brinson. Broken glass, fears, phobias, crying, sometimes desperate depressions—locked away in my "room" are all the jagged parts of my personality. Mrs. Brinson or Jean Brinson or just the child, Jeanie—they are all me! I accept them in degrees. They are what makes me an individual, different from any other on this earth. Sometimes I laugh at myself, often I cry, but I try to balance the two so that I never again will get confused as to who and what I am.

When I become Mrs. Brinson the bitch, I simply tell her to shut the hell up and leave my family alone. It really is that easy just to walk away and not hurt Gary or the boys.

Gary and I are still not only lovers, but also best friends. He is the best man I've ever known, and the only thing that exceeds my love for him, Monty and Shane, is my great thankfulness to them for staying with me throughout our ordeal. Gary's even learned how to drink beer moderately, taking his time and enjoying the taste.

I've lived through hell. In my memory are the images of much pain and sorrow, but I realize I made some of those problems myself. I missed out on much love and laughter with my own family, as well as with my brothers and sisters. My heart still aches for the suffering in my brother Robert's soul.

The year before mother became very ill, I took the train to see her in her beloved adopted state of New York. I was there about two weeks and we had many glorious laughs. Mother and I went shopping and to the beauty salon. I bought her some new clothes and saw a white long sleeved-blouse I adored, white being my favorite color. Dora was with us and said I was crazy if I paid forty-five dollars for that ruffled blouse. Mother said, "It's Jean's money, Dora." Then she turned to me. "If you want it that much, buy it, honey."

Dora didn't really mind. In fact, she laughed when I paid for the blouse.

On New Years Day, we got a phone call from Beth saying that Mother was very sick and in the hospital. No, it wasn't her heart. She had an infection of the brain—encephalitis. I had to get down the medical book to see what the word meant. Reading the explanation, I realized almost immediately that she could die from the disease.

In the next few weeks, my sisters and I talked by telephone almost every day so that they could explain her condition to me. For several days toward the end of January, I didn't hear from Beth and Dora. I assumed Mother was doing better.

Then, on January 30, the phone rang. Gary took the call. The girls had not phoned me earlier because of a pact Mother and I had made. Several years before, when she almost died from a heart attack, I had asked Mother to give me her promise that should she die before I did, no member of the family would call me. Mother gave her word, but only on the condition that I ask Gary and our sons to do the same should I be the first to die.

So the call that came that evening just after supper was for Gary, and not from one of my sisters, but from our son Monty. Dora had called him at the part-time job where he worked after school. The minute Gary looked at me so sadly, I knew Mother was dead.

Monty accompanied me on the train to Mother's. When we arrived, the ground of the old town she so loved was snow-covered. Dora and Will met us. Poor Will couldn't stop crying; I couldn't start.

All seven of Mother's children gathered in her small apartment to comfort each other and discuss the funeral. Mattie and Beth's husbands were present as well. The priest Dora had chosen had asked whether one of the children wanted to deliver Mother's eulogy. I was shocked when my other sisters and brothers unanimously chose me to be their spokesperson.

I stood honored and proud when the time came. I spoke of each of her children and how Mama had lived her entire life for us. I spoke of her marriage to Daddy and compared her life to the delicate yellow roses she so loved. I closed the eulogy with two sentences from Victor Hugo's "Les Miserables."

'It is a far better thing I do now than anything I've done before.

'It is a far better place I go now than any place I've gone before.'

Dora read Mother's simple will after the funeral. She had little material wealth to leave, but she spoke directly to each child. When it was my turn, her message was, "To you, Jean, I hope you find peace on this earth." After everyone else returned to their homes, Dora, Beth and I spent three weeks together going through Mother's belongings.

Her death brought to mind the fact that there is a part of me that I cannot explain to Gary or our sons. Somewhere within me lives Jeanie, the child, who used to call our mother "Mama." To that child who is part of the person I've become, "Mama" is forever young and beautiful, her silky white skin ever radiant, her long, flowing hair ever black as night. To Jeanie, she will never be old, wrinkled or gray.

After Mother's death, I finally told Robert what had happened that fateful night Daddy died. Robert came to our home one Thanksgiving Day. I held him in my arms and told him the truth. He cried as if a giant weight had been lifted from him. "I never hated you for beating Mama, but I nearly lost my mind wondering why you'd done it, or if it had been a dream." Robert needs counseling, but he's too proud to admit it. I don't fight his or my other sisters' and brothers' choices. They must decide their lives for themselves; it's enough that I love them and remember when we were so close.

You see, the brothers and sisters I know and cherish are still straggly youngins growing up on a tobacco farm. They are the children with dirty faces and feet whom I carried on my hips. I still love them as they were. To me, they were and are mine. They belong to Mama and me. I take great pride in having helped her raise them. It is their little children's faces I see when I think of them. They, like Jeanie, will never grow up. Maybe I refuse to allow them to because I need that memory in my life. It's a constant, just like the child in me.

Now, from my typing room window, looking out on the street, I see the railroad tracks leading north, south, east and west. Having gotten their schedules and watched them so many times, I know the destinations of all the trains. Life to me has been rather like these tracks on which the trains travel. They are like roads, crossroads, forks in the road, side roads and roads untraveled. Much of my life, I have either been forced down the wrong road or chosen it myself. Now, I think I've found the right one at last.

For the past twelve years, Gary, my first and greatest

love, and I have lived in this house. It is in the country, some twenty miles south of Charleston and seventy miles north of Savannah. I like to think of it as somewhere between Porgy 'n Bess and Carson McCullers country. My second greatest love in life is writing. I have completed my first book and sent it to my agent. I'm already at work on my second book, a novel. I pray that some day my work, like me, finds its place in the sun.

After moving to our new home, Gary and I went back to visit my birthplace in Horry County, to the old shack where it all happened: where Mama bore seven children, where Daddy beat us so unmercifully and died, where my brothers and sisters played in a mud-laden yard and hoped for better days, as all children do.

As I stood there, memories of those days washed over me. Looking around, I saw my family as they had been decades ago. All, except me, were gathered around the long, wooden table while Mama served dinner. Daddy was at the head of the table; Mama, at the other end. There were Dora and Mattie and Beth. There were Robert and Will and baby Tim. Only Jeanie was missing. As they ate and laughed, I noticed over in the corner a frightened, tearful little girl. It was me, Jeanie the child.

I walked softly toward her, took her trembling hand and brought her to her seat at the table. Then I walked around the family gathering to better take in Mama's wonderful Sunday dinner, the delicious smells of her food filling my senses. I began touching my brothers' and sisters' faces, one by one, each child I so deeply loved. Their love flowed through my veins. Then I came to Mama's chair. I reached down, gently pulled her black hair back and kissed the side of her beautiful face. Tears rolled down my cheeks and into my mouth. I called out each of their names and said I loved them, allowing the bittersweet taste of that time in all our lives to settle within me. But when I came to Daddy's chair and reached down to touch him, he disappeared like a ghost. I stood there for a long while; then, I went back outside to Gary.

As I took his hand, I felt something begin to grow inside of me. It came slowly at first, like the beauty of the rising sun, but has grown more each day of my life. The wonderment of it still leaves me breathless. It's the most simple of things, yet so rare. It's called peace. At long last, I had peace in my soul.

Not long ago, before this book went to press, Gary and I received a phone call. The old shack where I'd lived with Mama, Daddy, my sisters and brothers, had been torn down. At first, I didn't want to see the final, grim reminder of that painful time. Later, I changed my mind. Once there, I stood amazed. Where the rotting shack had once stood, rich, green, fragrant grass now thrived.

Looking around, I seemed to see the footprints of little Jeanie's bare feet etched in the rich loam. I know she's still there. She will be there for all eternity, but I think she's happy now. At last she's finally found her home, a place where she belongs.